Cheaters never win . . .

Drew shrugged. "I gotta check to see if it can handle the heavy equipment. For after they catch the cheaters."

Cheaters! Elizabeth got to her feet, her heart hammering. If they found out that she'd cheated, what would they do?

"Did he say . . . cheated?" Sophia croaked.

Elizabeth had forgotten about her friend. She whirled around. Stay calm, Elizabeth ordered herself. "Cheated!" she blustered. "Who would do something dumb like that? Didn't they know they'd spoil the dance for everybody?" Her voice sounded shaky and cracked to her, but maybe Sophia wouldn't notice.

"I c-can't imagine who would do that. C-Can you?" Sophia asked. Elizabeth could see Sophia's knees trembling.

"N-No, I can't," Elizabeth croaked. "Of course, I'm innocent," she lied.

"Oh, so am I," Sophia said, sounding shocked that anyone would even consider accusing her. "I'm, like, a hundred percent innocent. Two hundred percent."

There was silence. Elizabeth felt she should say something more. "Cheating!" she exclaimed. "And in a TV game show too! What is this world coming to?"

"They ought to be, um, tossed in jail for all eternity," Sophia said with feeling, her eyes darting anxiously left and right.

Elizabeth sighed loudly. "They certainly should be," she added, crossing her fingers behind her back just in case.

Visit the Official Sweet Valley Web Site on the Internet at:

http://www.sweetvalley.com

SWEET VALLEY TWINS

The Boyfriend Mess

◇

Written by
Jamie Suzanne

Created by
FRANCINE PASCAL

BANTAM BOOKS
NEW YORK·TORONTO·LONDON·SYDNEY·AUCKLAND

To Coral Cuthbersan

RL 4, 008-012

THE BOYFRIEND MESS

A Bantam Book / March 1998

*Sweet Valley High® and Sweet Valley Twins® are
registered trademarks of Francine Pascal.*

Conceived by Francine Pascal.

*Produced by Daniel Weiss Associates, Inc.
33 West 17th Street
New York, NY 10011.*

Cover art by Bruce Emmett.

ISBN: 0-553-48598-9

Published simultaneously in the United States and Canada

*Bantam Books are published by Bantam Books, a division of Bantam
Doubleday Dell Publishing Group, Inc. Its trademark, consisting of the
words "Bantam Books" and the portrayal of a rooster, is Registered in the
U.S. Patent and Trademark Office and in other countries. Marca
Registrada. Bantam Books, 1540 Broadway, New York, New York 10036.*

PRINTED IN THE UNITED STATES OF AMERICA

OPM   0 9 8 7 6 5 4 3 2 1

One

◇

You should be happy, Jessica Wakefield told herself as she leaned gloomily against the high concrete wall in the Sweet Valley Middle School parking lot.

Jessica had a lot to be happy about. It was Valentine's Day, her very favorite day of the entire year. Next to Christmas, of course. And maybe New Year's. And the first day of summer vacation. But it was her very favorite day, besides those.

On top of that, she was going to spend the entire day at Dizzy Planet, the great new amusement park that had been built just outside Sweet Valley, California, where she lived. Jessica had been aching to go for weeks and weeks, and now she finally had her chance. She tried to smile as she thought of the great rides she'd only heard about: the Antigravity Galaxy, where it seemed as though the whole world dropped out from under you as the ride spun around; the Monster Splash water ride; the Space Demon roller coaster.

Jessica nodded. Today was her chance to get back at her so-called best friend, Lila Fowler, who'd been to Dizzy Planet the day it opened and hadn't shut up about it since.

"Attention, please!" a woman's voice boomed out from a van across the parking lot. Even though it was pretty early on a Saturday morning, the lot was jammed with students, most of them crowding around the van.

"OK!" the woman bellowed. "I'm Jane Sylvester, assistant to Byron Miller, the hunkiest game show host in the universe! And I get paid big money to say that, so I know it's true. All the winning couples for *Young Love*, over here on the double!"

Young Love. Jessica wrinkled her nose and looked down at her bright yellow T-shirt, which bore the logo of the popular TV show on which contestants competed to win dates with their ideal match. Young Love! the shirt trumpeted in red letters, and underneath the logo it added, Check Your Local Listings. The same logo was printed on the side of the van.

Jessica sighed again. She was actually half of a winning couple on *Young Love. This is exactly what I wanted*, she reminded herself, tugging on the tip of her long blond ponytail. *How can I complain? Valentine's Day, the amusement park, and* Young Love.

"I mean *now!*" Ms. Sylvester's voice carried across the parking lot.

Jessica knew she should move. But her feet wouldn't let her. There was a gnawing feeling in the pit of her stomach—

"Jess!"

Jessica jumped. "What is it?" she blurted out, then clamped a hand over her mouth. Every nerve in her body seemed to be stretched to its limit. Then she recognized her twin sister, Elizabeth, and breathed deeply. Elizabeth was safe. Elizabeth was the only one who knew her secret. "Why are you scaring me to death?" she snapped.

"Better hurry." Elizabeth smiled nervously at her twin.

Jessica glared. With a groan, she straightened up and took a few small steps forward.

"Now listen, Jess." Elizabeth's fingers grasped Jessica's wrist. "When you see Todd, it's really important that you be nice to him, OK? I mean, it's Valentine's Day, and he thinks he's going to Dizzy Planet with *me*. You don't have to be all lovey-dovey with him or anything, but you do have to be nice." She looked Jessica full in the face. "OK?"

Jessica stared stonily at her twin. It was like looking into a mirror. Both girls had long blond hair and blue-green eyes. A dimple even showed in the same cheek when they smiled. They looked so much alike, even their friends sometimes had trouble telling them apart when they dressed the same.

But inside, the two girls were as different as could be. Jessica lived for parties, shopping, fashion, and boy talk. She was a member of the exclusive Unicorn Club at school, and she was happiest in a large group of kids. Preferably cool ones. Elizabeth, on the other hand, was quieter and more thoughtful. Writing and reading were her favorite activities, though she always made time for her family and her own friends.

Jessica sighed loudly. It was amazing that two people as different as she and Elizabeth could get along so well most of the time.

Most of the time.

"Look, I'm *sorry*," Elizabeth hissed, craning her neck to see the van. "I mean it, I really am. Especially after . . . well . . ." Her voice trailed off. "Never mind. It's just that—that you *have* to be nice to him."

"I know," Jessica snapped. She wished her sister would stop talking. *It's all your fault anyway*, she thought, trying to ignore the knot in her stomach.

And it *was* Elizabeth's fault, she assured herself. When *Young Love* chose Sweet Valley Middle School to be on an episode, Elizabeth had been selected as a contestant. She was supposed to pick out her ideal date from a mystery panel of three guys from school. Only Elizabeth had chickened out and gotten Jessica to take her place, pretending to be Elizabeth.

Which, Jessica thought morosely, had been a really bad idea. Because the guy she'd picked had been Todd Wilkins. Not that she had anything against Todd, exactly. He was nice enough and all that. But he was kind of, well . . . boring. Yeah, boring. That was the word.

And he was Elizabeth's sort-of boyfriend.

Her mind flashed back to what had happened next. Jessica couldn't help wincing; she'd never been so embarrassed in her entire life. Elizabeth had gotten up onstage a little later as one of the mystery girls for Aaron Dallas, Jessica's own sort-of boyfriend, and pretended to be Jessica. She made Jessica look like a total airhead—on national TV! And now the *Young Love* staff was treating the winning couples to a day at the amusement park, followed by a dance for all the students later on that night, and Aaron Dallas was going with Amy Sutton.

And Jessica Wakefield not only had to pose as her twin sister, but she was stuck with Todd "Boring" Wilkins too.

Life just wasn't fair.

Elizabeth twisted a lock of hair. "If I'd known Todd was going to be in that group, I'd have stuck with it."

Jessica didn't care. She glanced at her sister, seeing the monogrammed *JW* on Elizabeth's purple shirt. *My purple shirt*, she reminded herself. But it was important that nobody think Elizabeth was really Elizabeth. She quickened her pace toward the van.

"Hi, Elizabeth!"

Jessica stopped short. Todd Wilkins stood directly in front of her, smiling shyly. She glanced toward her sister, but remembered just in time that she was Elizabeth today. "Hi, Todd," she said, not bothering to smile back.

Elizabeth poked Jessica in the side.

Jessica gritted her teeth and pasted a humongous

grin on her face. "Hi, Todd!" she said heartily.

"Don't act ridiculous," Elizabeth whispered.

"Oh, cut it out, Jess, you're always bugging me," Jessica said brightly, enjoying the moment.

Todd's smile widened. He smoothed out his own *Young Love* T-shirt. "For a minute I thought you weren't even going to say hello!" he said. "Look, I got new sneaks for the occasion." He rolled up his pants legs, showing Jessica black shoes with orange laces.

How nerdy can you get? Jessica thought, trying not to roll her eyes. "They're, um, real nice, Todd," she lied, forcing another smile. *Think like Elizabeth.* "Very . . . practical."

"Helloooooo, Sweet Valley!"

Jessica whirled around. Byron Miller, the teenage host of *Young Love,* was standing on top of the van, microphone in his hand, smiling a dazzling smile. "Helloooooo, Sweet Valley!" he repeated, thrusting one arm into the air like a heavyweight boxer. "Are you ready for *looooove?*"

A few kids in the front row cheered, and Ellen Riteman screeched, "Yes!" at the top of her lungs.

Byron's grin grew more brilliant. He patted down his shock of beautiful brown hair. Jessica couldn't take her eyes off him. He seemed even cuter today than he had during the taping of the show. "I can't *heeeeear* you!" he teased, cupping one hand to his ear.

"Yes!" the kids chorused. Winston Egbert put two fingers in his mouth and whistled.

"Sweet Valley!" Byron gestured to the audience.

"The most romaaaantic town in the West! Today we'll see if our contestants chose dream dates—" He paused dramatically. "Or if they chose *scream* dates."

"I know what you chose, Elizabeth," Todd said with a smile, stepping closer to Jessica.

Jessica barely noticed. She was admiring Byron—his hair, his sparkling dark eyes, his chiseled face and jaw, his poise. Her heart quickened. Byron was only a couple of years older than she was. Jessica hadn't made a very good first impression on him at the taping. But today she would have a chance to make up for it.

Byron's gaze swept across the crowd. "There's Amy Sutton," he said into the mike. "Will she have a great time with her mystery date, Aaron Dallas? Or will it be splitsville before they even get to the Tunnel of a Thousand Smooches?"

"Aaron and Amy!" Winston shouted, clapping rhythmically. "Sittin' in a tree! K-I-S-S-I-N—"

"Grow up, Egbert!" Aaron called out. "We're not in third grade anymore. At least, the *rest* of us aren't!"

Amy gave Aaron a grateful smile.

"Or Elizabeth Wakefield," Byron went on, his eyes connecting suddenly with Jessica's. Jessica felt her throat instantly go dry. "I tell you what, Mr. Todd Wilkins . . ." He paused and winked playfully. "If you're scared to take your lovely date on the Space Demon today, I'll take her off your hands!"

Todd turned red as the crowd erupted into cries of "Go, Todd!"

"First comes love!" Winston chanted. "Then comes marriage!"

"What a jerk," Elizabeth whispered.

Jessica breathed deeply. She suddenly felt light-headed. *I'll take her off your hands.* Those had been Byron Miller's exact words. And what had he called her? *Lovely.* That was it. *Your lovely date.* The phrase echoed through Jessica's head. The hunkiest TV host in the entire *universe* had just called her "lovely."

Byron snapped his fingers. The *Young Love* theme music boomed out across the parking lot.

"Um—Elizabeth?" Todd placed a hand lightly on her shoulder.

Jessica shook him off and leaned forward, her eyes glittering as she stared at Byron.

Maybe, just maybe, this day would turn out all right after all.

"Let's see." Ms. Sylvester's eyes scanned a list. She sat at a table outside the van, a pen in her hand. "Who's here who's supposed to be here? Is there an Elizabeth Whackfield in the house?"

Elizabeth stood nearby, scanning the crowd of couples dejectedly. *I could have spent the whole day with Todd at Dizzy Planet*, she reminded herself. But instead, Todd was going with Jessica.

Life just wasn't fair.

It was partly Byron Miller's fault. Byron liked to crack jokes at the expense of the contestants on the show, and Elizabeth hadn't thought she could deal with that. So she'd gotten Jessica to take her place—and Jessica had picked Todd. So, in a way, it was Byron's fault.

But it was Jessica's fault too, she reminded herself. Jessica had flat-out *refused* to change back after the taping was over. Even though she was going to Dizzy Planet with Elizabeth's sort-of boyfriend.

She swallowed hard.

The problem was that, deep down, Elizabeth half suspected it was really all her own fault. She'd gone on the show, pretending to be Jessica, and had given totally ditzy responses to the questions Aaron had asked. Her plan had been to try not to get picked—or picked on—at any price. Unfortunately, the only way to do that had been to make Jessica out to be a real idiot. Elizabeth narrowed her eyes, angry at herself for not giving good answers. If she had, then Jessica wouldn't be so mad at her. And maybe Aaron would have picked her, and then they would both be going to Dizzy Planet, and it would have been easy to switch back. Oh, why hadn't she thought of that sooner?

Elizabeth sighed and took a quick look at her sister, who was staring up at Byron Miller with a dreamy expression. She wished with all her heart that she'd done things differently. But now . . . well, it was too late. She couldn't imagine herself trying to talk to Jessica about switching back now.

"Elizabeth? Elizabeth Whackfield?" Ms. Sylvester repeated. "I gotta be honest with you guys. Every winning couple has to go to Dizzy Planet. Every winning couple has to come back together." Her stare traveled around the group of contestants. "Otherwise tonight's dance is *history*. So, how about it? Where's Whackfield?"

Todd cleared his throat. "She means you," he said, and nudged Jessica.

"Huh?" Jessica leaped as if she'd been stung. "What do you think you're doing, Todd?"

Todd's face fell. He looked uncertainly at Jessica. "She called your name," he explained. "You don't have to bite my head off." Todd tugged Jessica's hand. "But I think we're supposed to get on the van now."

"Hold on," Jessica snapped crossly, pulling away. "You don't have to be on my case every minute, OK? I'm not ready yet."

"I just—" Todd clamped his mouth shut. Bowing his head, he turned away from the van and kicked at the pavement. His shoulders sagged.

Elizabeth's did too. So much for her reminders to her sister about being nice to Todd.

She wished she'd never bothered to get out of bed. No, she wished she'd never been born. This was looking to be one of the worst days in the history of the world.

Not only was Jessica getting to go to Dizzy Planet instead of her, but now it looked as if she was going to make sure Todd never wanted to speak to Elizabeth again.

And there wasn't a thing Elizabeth could do about it.

Two

◇

"Donald Nerdling!" Ms. Sylvester boomed out. "And Janet Howl! Owooooo!"

Maria Slater stifled a laugh. She suspected that Ms. Sylvester was mangling the names on purpose. *But "Janet Howl"—that one was pretty good.* Smiling broadly, Maria looked around for her own partner, Patrick Morris. She hoped they'd be called next. She was totally psyched for this trip and for the dance that night!

Donald Zwerdling beamed up at Janet from beneath his red hair. He offered Janet his arm, but she elbowed him rudely out of the way. With an angry glare on her face, she stalked over to Ms. Sylvester. "I'm Janet," she snapped.

"I will never understand how those two ended up together," Amy Sutton muttered to Maria.

"Poor Donald," Maria muttered back. Janet Howell, an eighth grader who was president of the Unicorn Club, was not exactly one of her favorite people. Ever since Maria had moved to Sweet Valley a few months earlier from Hollywood, where she'd been a child actress, her path had crossed Janet's more times than she cared to remember. Nobody deserved to get stuck spending a whole day with Janet. "It's too bad that Donald has to put up with her," she remarked as Donald joined Janet at the table.

"Really," Amy agreed, wiping her long straight hair away from her face. "I knew I should have worn a headband! Actually, I'd trade partners with Janet in a minute, even if Donald is kind of a dweeb. Donald's smart. And polite. Meanwhile, *I* get stuck with Aaron Dallas." She rolled her eyes.

"Zwerdling," Donald told Ms. Sylvester. "Z-W-E-R . . ."

"I know what you mean," Maria agreed sympathetically. Too often Aaron was goofy, loud, or just plain rude, although he meant well.

Amy grimaced. "The first thing he said to me today was, 'Hey, Ame!'" Amy dropped her voice almost an octave in imitation of Aaron. "'Ready to hit the Tunnel of Loooooove?' Then he made these smooching noises, and everybody laughed. . . ." Her voice trailed off. "Even Ken."

Ken Matthews was Amy's sort-of boyfriend. Maria wrinkled her nose. "That's tough," she said.

"*Zwerd*ling," Donald told Ms. Sylvester. "With a Z. As in zirconium."

Amy shrugged. "I guess boys will be boys. Or Aarons will be Aarons, anyway." She shook her head. "Then he said he was going to buy five cotton candies, eat them one right after the other, and ride the roller coaster till he threw up."

"A thrill a minute," Maria observed. "If I live to be a hundred, I'll never understand guys."

"You're not kidding," Amy said with a sigh. "I thought about not going, but then the whole school wouldn't get to have the dance. Although I'm really worried about having to spend the day with him *and* be his date to the dance." She wrapped a lock of hair around her finger. "Actually, he didn't want to go with *me* either. He said he wanted to go with Jessica, or Janet or Ellen or somebody. I was his fifty-third choice."

"He *told* you that?" Maria was shocked.

"Sure." Amy managed a grin. "So I told him he was my eighty-fifth choice, and he got mad. Oh, we're going to have a *great* time." She took a deep breath. "So—are you psyched to be going with Patrick?"

Maria nodded vigorously. "Yeah, it's going to be really cool." She remembered the excitement she'd felt back in the *Young Love* studios when Patrick had called out her number to be his mystery dream date. "It's not that I've got a crush on him or anything," she added quickly. "It's just that—"

"You'd better not," Amy teased, "if you want to stay friends with Sophia."

"*Zwerdling,*" Donald was still saying desperately. Janet's eyes flashed and she turned away from the table in disgust. "Z as in Zwerdling. W as in Zwerdling. E as in Zwerdling—"

Maria grinned. Sophia Rizzo was one of her closest friends, and she knew very well that Sophia and Patrick were sort of an item. "It's just that Patrick's such a nice guy," she said. "And popular." She pictured Patrick in her mind. Blue eyes, curly hair, a really nice smile . . .

"Uh-huh," Amy said dryly. "Since when do you care about popular?"

Maria stroked her chin. "It's hard to explain," she said slowly. "I guess . . . it has to do with being new. Because I just moved to Sweet Valley and everything." She thought hard. "Being friends with you and Sophia and Elizabeth has been great, but sometimes I wonder about the other kids. You know—if they like me only because I was once a movie star."

"Oh, *Zwerdling!*" Ms. Sylvester finally bellowed. "Why didn't you say so? Sign on the dotted line." She shoved a piece of paper at Donald, who rolled his eyes.

"We're probably next," Amy said in a flat voice.

"I guess I feel like being picked by Patrick means I really belong," Maria went on. "Patrick didn't know it was me behind that curtain. He didn't like me because I used to be in the movies. He wasn't worried that I was a selfish, spoiled brat, the way some kids did. He liked me for . . . well, for *me*."

"Who's next?" Ms. Sylvester shouted as Donald trotted after Janet to board the van. "Aha! Amy Shudder and Aaron Dullest!"

Amy threw Maria a pained look. "Wish me luck. I'm going to need it."

"Luck!" Maria called after her friend. *Aaron Dullest*, she thought, and smiled. That one was pretty good too.

It was actually kind of weird, the way the other couples weren't looking forward to this trip. Aaron and Amy weren't getting along. Janet hated Donald's guts. Even Elizabeth seemed to be tired of Todd already. Maria stifled a giggle as she thought about how they would all look at the Valentine's Day dance that night.

But Maria was another story. Being picked by Patrick, sight unseen, had made her day. For the first time since she'd come to Sweet Valley, she felt as though she truly belonged.

This was going to be the best day of the year.

"I just wish you'd paid more attention," Sophia Rizzo said softly. She twisted her hands nervously and craned her neck to make sure no one was listening. Her heart was beating at least three times normal speed. What if somebody had gotten suspicious and hidden a microphone somewhere near the van?

Patrick Morris shrugged and scuffed the toe of his

tennis shoe on the blacktop. "Yeah, well," he muttered awkwardly, not meeting Sophia's eyes, "I tried."

"I know." Sophia glanced up to the roof of the van. Luckily Byron Miller wasn't looking their way. "I just wish you'd remembered the . . ." Her voice drifted off. *Better not say it*, she decided. *Just in case.* "The you-know-what," she hissed.

"Like I said." Patrick straightened up and swept his thick brown hair off his forehead. His *Young Love* T-shirt billowed in the breeze, too big for his thin body. "I tried. And I'm sorry. But I'm kind of stuck with Maria now. I mean, what do you want me to do? Tell her?" He leaned toward an imaginary girl to his left. "Gee, Maria," he said in a deep voice, "there's something you've got to know. I picked you by—"

"Shhh!" Sophia's heart pounded in her chest. Frantically she reached forward and covered Patrick's mouth with her hand before he could blurt out the word *mistake*.

Patrick pulled Sophia's wrist away. "I can't tell her that," he said wearily. "It would hurt her feelings."

Jealousy welled up in Sophia. "How about *my* feelings?" she asked.

With all her heart Sophia wished that she and Patrick hadn't tried to cheat in the *Young Love* game. They'd agreed on a question that Patrick would ask all three candidates. Sophia would give a certain answer, so he'd know who to pick.

But Patrick had gotten the question mixed up. And all three candidates had given similar answers. So

Patrick had guessed—and guessed wrong. Instead of Sophia, he'd wound up with Maria.

And ever since they'd hatched their plot, Sophia hadn't been sleeping well. She'd had nightmares about being arrested. She was sure that cheating on TV was a really serious crime. One episode of *Homicide Plus!* had showed a guy who'd been sentenced to thirty years in jail for cheating.

Or maybe that was the guy who'd robbed the bank and thrown the teller off a cliff.

Either way, Sophia was on edge. It was only a question of time before the FBI or the CIA or the Secret Service or whoever it was caught up with her, and then . . .

She swallowed hard. "What about *me?*" she asked plaintively.

"What *about* you?" Patrick smiled broadly and reached for Sophia's hand. "Look, Maria's just a friend."

Sophia nodded, not trusting herself to speak. She let her hand be enveloped in Patrick's firm grip. Maybe Patrick was right—

A shadow fell on the wall of the van. Sophia gasped. Every muscle in her body froze. It was a police officer, she felt certain. She braced herself for the clink of the handcuffs on her wrists.

"Um, hi." A tall blond boy stood there, his hands thrust deep into his back pockets. He wore a *Young Love* shirt, but a blue one, not a yellow one like Patrick's, and baggy jeans. "Excuse me for interrupting. I was just wondering—"

"No problem." Patrick nodded to the boy, dropping Sophia's hand. "What's up?"

The boy smiled and ran his hand through his hair. He looked a little embarrassed. Sophia began to relax. He certainly didn't act like any cop she'd seen on TV. Anyway, he was too young—only about her age. "I'm Marshall," he said shyly. "I'm a relative of Byron Miller's. His, um, cousin."

Sophia held her breath. That could be just as bad as a cop. "Were you listening to our conversation?" she demanded.

Marshall frowned. "Huh? No, I wasn't listening. I was watching that girl over there. In the *Young Love* shirt." He stabbed his forefinger toward the van, where Maria was standing.

"You mean Maria?" Patrick raised an eyebrow. "With the dark hair?"

"Um, yeah." Marshall smiled crookedly. "Listen, this might sound weird, but she looks really familiar to me. I think I might know her, but I can't remember how. I was wondering if maybe you knew her and could introduce me."

Sophia felt air whoosh out of her lungs. So Marshall was just looking at Maria. Well, that was innocent enough.

Patrick smiled, showing his even teeth. Sophia relaxed, admiring the way Patrick looked when he grinned. He had a killer smile, no doubt about it. "Maria's a friend of ours," he said, emphasizing the word *friend* slightly. "I think we could manage that. C'mon." He turned to Sophia. "What'd I tell you?" he mouthed to her.

"I guess you're right," Sophia murmured, watching as Patrick tapped Maria on the shoulder and introduced her to Marshall. From the look on Maria's face, it was clear that she was delighted to meet Marshall—which meant that Sophia didn't have to worry about Maria taking Patrick away from her.

That was one big load off her mind.

Now if I can only stop worrying about the police, I'll be all set! she told herself.

"I, um, just kind of noticed you," Marshall said hesitantly. He stuck out one hand and hitched up his jeans with the other. "And I thought that I knew you somehow. Do I look familiar to you too?" He grinned at Maria nervously.

Marshall was awfully cute, Maria thought. She stuck out her own hand and shook his. His grip was strong but not too strong. She caught Marshall's eye and held his gaze for just a second. "Well, um, to be honest—no," she said. "But I guess I know you now."

"Well, that's good enough for me," Marshall said earnestly.

"So, do you live in Sweet Valley?" Maria asked.

"No," Marshall replied. "I'm just visiting. I'm here with Byron, my—uh—cousin." He paused and looked uncomfortable. Then he added, "Actually, I feel a little weird about telling people that he's my cousin, because sometimes they kind of cozy up to me once they know I'm related to Byron. They think I can get 'em on the show." He made a face. "Sometimes it's kind of hard to tell who likes me for me. But I guess you wouldn't know about that."

You'd be surprised, Maria thought, her eyes dancing. But she decided not to say anything just yet. "That must be tough," she agreed. "So . . . what kinds of things are you interested in?"

"Oh, a lot of stuff." Marshall thought a minute. "Um, movies, mostly. Baseball, some. And model cars. But mostly movies."

Maria raised her eyebrows. "What kind of movies?"

"All kinds," Marshall said with a huge lop-sided grin. He adjusted the collar of his T-shirt. "I'm just a big movie fan. I watch 'em all. Comedies, epics, dramas, action-adventure—you name it, I've probably seen it." He coughed. "But, hey, enough about me. How about you, Maria? What do you like to do?"

"Well, I like movies too," Maria said slowly, not sure that she wanted to tell Marshall about her acting career, no matter how nice he seemed. "What's your very favorite movie? Of all time, I mean."

Marshall looked off into space, at a spot just beyond Maria's left shoulder. "If I had to choose just one . . ." He made a clicking noise with his tongue and pulled his pants up again. "I guess I'd have to pick . . . um, *Bald Eagle Landing*."

Maria leaned forward, her heart beating furiously.

"*Bald Eagle Landing*?" she burst out. "You mean the original or—"

Marshall waved his hand in the air. "No, no, the remake," he said, shaking his head. "Why? Do you know it?"

"Well—" Maria bit her lip. The truth was, she'd had a part in the remake. *If he's got a relative in show business, he'll understand,* a little voice in her head told her. But another part of her still hesitated. "Um—you could say that."

"Wait a minute." Marshall narrowed his eyes and stared at her intently. Then he backed up a couple of steps and held out his finger and thumb as if trying to see her face between them. After a moment he broke into a huge smile. "You were *in* that, weren't you? You played . . . who was it? The youngest Evans girl. No wonder you look so familiar!"

Maria laughed nervously. So the secret was out. "Guilty," she said, raising her arms in mock surrender. "You must really be a movie fan if you recognized—"

"Oh, hey, don't give me that!" Marshall looked astonished. "I mean, you're famous. Maria Slater, right? Sure, I saw you in a bunch of things. Like, um, *The Visitor.* And *Mansion of Blood.*" He looked at her curiously. "So, what are you doing in Sweet Valley?"

Maria smiled. "I'm retired," she said.

"Cool!" Marshall grinned back. "Bet you wanted a more normal life, huh? My, um, cousin keeps talking about doing the same thing."

Maria breathed deeply. It sure sounded as if

Marshall understood. As if he knew that being a movie star wasn't really anything special—that it could be a royal pain sometimes. "Yeah, it was getting in the way of my social life," she said.

"I know what you mean," Marshall agreed. "You're so much more interesting as a whole person anyway, don't you think? Byron says—well, never mind what Byron says. So how do you like Sweet Valley?"

Maria didn't hesitate. "I love it," she said with feeling. She could hear Marshall's words echoing through her head: *"You're so much more interesting as a whole person."* Her palms grew damp. *When he said "you," did he mean me personally?* "Sweet Valley is a really cool place."

"Finding friends you can relate to?" Marshall asked, lifting an eyebrow.

Maria loved the way he looked with that eyebrow up in the air. "You bet," she agreed, thinking of Patrick. And Sophia and Elizabeth and Amy and all the kids who, she was positive now, liked her for herself and not just because she used to be a movie star. "There are lots of nice kids here."

Marshall's ears turned faintly pink. "Well, if the kids here are all as nice and smart as you, I can believe it."

"That's so sweet!" Maria's heart leaped. "Thanks so much for the compliment, Marshall."

"Next!" Ms. Sylvester brayed. She checked her list. "Maria See-ya-later and Patrick Morose!"

Maria's face fell. She had forgotten all about the trip to Dizzy Planet. And although she really wanted to go, she wished she could get to know Marshall a little bit better. But now she'd never see him again, probably. "I'd better go," she murmured.

"Oh, you're going on the trip?" Marshall sounded surprised.

Maria nodded. "How long are you in town for?" she asked. "Will you be at the dance tonight?"

Marshall hitched up his pants again and smoothed back his hair. "Better than that," he told her. "I'm coming along to Dizzy Planet too."

"You are?" Maria's mouth opened wide. She knew she probably looked like a fish, but she didn't care. "Cool!"

I take back what I said about this being the best day of the year, she thought as she stepped toward Ms. Sylvester's table.

This could be the very best day of my entire life!

Three

"What do you *mean*, you're not going?" Ms. Sylvester asked, staring hard at Janet Howell.

"Just what I said." Janet slouched in the front of the van, her arms folded in front of her chest. She turned to glare at Donald, who sat downcast in his seat. "I'm not going. At least, not with that *nerd*."

"Fine with me," Donald said.

"'Fine with *me*,'" Janet mimicked. "Either you let me switch," she said in a low voice, staring daggers at Ms. Sylvester, "or I am leaving this van right now and I'm not kidding. Do you know what he just did?"

Jessica leaned into the aisle to see better. This sounded interesting. Anyway, Todd kept trying to put his arm around her, and his face went all goofy-looking whenever he did that, and Jessica was certain she was going to punch him in the nose if he kept it up. Or else break out in hysterical fits of giggles. "What?" she asked curiously.

"He's describing the life cycle of the praying mantis!" Janet snarled, clenching her fists. "I mean, give me a *break*."

"I thought you'd be interested," Donald said mildly. "How the female bites the head off the male and—"

Janet slapped her hands over her ears. "See what I mean?"

Jessica grinned. She wondered if Donald was trying to send Janet a not-so-subtle message about her behavior.

"So how about it?" Janet said sharply. "Can I switch with someone? Amy, maybe? Or even Elizabeth?"

Elizabeth? Startled, Jessica swiveled around to see what her sister was doing on the van. "Where's—" she began, but then realized the mistake she was about to make.

What would Elizabeth say? "You can't switch with *me*," she said. Todd smiled.

Ms. Sylvester stared hard at Janet over the tops of her sunglasses. "You can't switch with anybody. It's in the rules. Anyway, we're pulling out in two minutes."

"Then you're pulling out without me." Janet took a tiny step forward.

"Oh, Byron!" Ms. Sylvester lifted her head and called through the sunroof of the van. "There's a young lady here who wants out. You want to throw her to the wolves, or should I?"

There was a scuffling noise. Jessica looked up. Byron Miller's feet appeared in the open sunroof. "Cowabunga!" he cried, dropping lightly into the aisle.

Jessica raised her eyebrows, impressed. Byron was obviously both strong and graceful. She was sure that not even Aaron could have done that maneuver without falling on his face.

"Oh, I'll do the honors," Byron said with his suave grin. "Which one?"

Ms. Sylvester pointed. "Her. Janet Howl-at-the-moon."

"Aha." Byron drew a handheld microphone out of his pocket. Jessica watched curiously as he flicked the switch to on. "Sweet Valley Middle School!" he said in his best host's voice. "Can you heeeeeear me?" He flashed Jessica a brilliant grin, showing all his teeth.

"Yeah!" the kids outside the van chorused.

"We have a situation here," Byron continued. "Miss Janet Howell is refusing to go with the partner she picked. Now, if that's her decision, I'll certainly respect it, but there's a consequence." There was a pause. Then Byron barked into the microphone. "Do you know what happens if Janet walks, Sweet Valley?"

"What?" the crowd of kids yelled back.

"Then tonight's dance is *toast!*" Byron cried out happily. "*Sayonara*, finished, good-bye! *Young Love* will find some other school that really *wants* a dance." Janet flinched. Byron put a hand casually on her shoulder. "So what do you think, Sweet Valley? Do you want Janet to leave this van?"

"No way!" the kids called back to him. Jessica could make out a smattering of boos.

"Down with Janet!" Winston Egbert yelled.

Byron grinned, obviously enjoying himself. "Rules are rules," he said, his voice booming across the parking lot. "So Janet, my friend, it's up to you. You can walk off this van and face all your former friends out there. Or you can stay here with Donald." He thrust the microphone three inches from Janet's mouth. "So what's the answer, Jan?"

"She'll walk," Todd guessed, his arm snaking around Jessica's shoulders.

Jessica shrugged him off. "No, she won't," she replied. No way would Janet get off the van now. The Janet she knew would rather take poison than have the whole school mad at her. Even if it meant going to the theme park with Donald.

Todd gave her a funny look. "How can you be sure?"

Jessica's heart raced. *Dummy!* she told herself. How many times now had she nearly blown her cover? "Oh—I guess I've listened to Jessica talk about Queen Janet so many times, I feel like I really know her," she explained.

Which was true, as far as it went.

Todd laughed. "Queen Janet," he said. "That's about right."

Jessica only smiled. When you came right down to it, she wasn't sorry to see Janet embarrassed like this. Janet could be so *overbearing* sometimes.

"Stay! Stay! Stay!" the kids outside the van chanted.

Janet clenched her fists. "Oh, all *right*," she snarled at last, as though she was doing everybody else a favor.

"Phew!" Todd wiped his forehead. "I don't know what your sister sees in Janet. She can be so *overbearing* sometimes."

Jessica felt a surge of irritation. So what if it was true? Todd had no business saying it. "Oh, Janet's got her good points," she murmured, flouncing in her seat and staring out the opposite window from Todd.

"She does?" Todd looked surprised.

"Well, a couple of them, anyway," Jessica amended. "Two or three." How she hated being Elizabeth. With any luck, soon after they got to Dizzy Planet she'd lose him accidentally on purpose. But for now she'd just have to play along. She aimed a nauseatingly sweet smile at Todd.

Todd smiled back. "That's one of the things I've always appreciated about you, Elizabeth," he said. His face did that goofy thing again. "You're able to see the good in everybody. Even *her*." He motioned toward Janet with his thumb.

If I have to keep staring at him like this, I'm going to throw up, Jessica told herself, smiling harder. "Oh, you're so sweet, Todd," she murmured, leaning a little farther away in case he tried to kiss her or something gross like that. She'd shared a kiss with Aaron once, but Todd—no way.

"Ready to roll?" Byron flicked the mike off and looked around the van. His gaze lit upon Jessica. "Hey, Elizabeth!" he said. "Mind if I share a seat with you and your boyfriend?"

That was easy. "I don't mind at all!" Jessica said, sliding over to make room.

How could I ever have thought today would turn out to be a bummer? she wondered as Byron sat down, flashing her his trademark grin.

"Where do you want this bunting?" Sophia asked. The van was about to pull out, and she had gone into the gym to help the *Young Love* staff hang the decorations for the Valentine dance that evening. Some other kids were helping too.

The *Young Love* staffer motioned to the top of the bleachers. "Up there, where that blond girl's standing."

Sophia turned. "You mean Elizabeth?" she asked, catching sight of—

No, wait. Sophia checked herself. *Weird.* Sophia frowned. Not that you could really tell the difference, but just from the way the girl was standing, Sophia would have guessed it was Elizabeth.

But obviously it wasn't.

"Hi, Jessica!" Sophia called up, grabbing the bunting and heading up the bleachers, but Jessica didn't turn around.

Well, that wasn't surprising. They weren't exactly friends anyway. Sophia let her thoughts drift off to Patrick. Her heart thudded. He'd been sitting in the back row of the van, with Maria and Marshall. Patrick had been leaning against the window, yawning, while Maria and Marshall talked up a storm. Not that Sophia was an expert on these things, but it sure looked as if Marshall and Maria were hitting it off. Well, more power to Maria. Marshall might look a little awkward, but he obviously had a nice personality. "Yeah, chemistry!" she quoted from her favorite musical, *Guys and Dolls*, as she arrived at the top of the steps.

Elizabeth whirled around. "Oh, hi, Sophia," she said. "You startled me!"

"Sorry," Sophia murmured. Now that she looked closely, she could tell it wasn't Elizabeth. The *JW* monogram on the shirt was a dead giveaway, for one thing. It was strange how different the twins were; though Elizabeth was one of her best friends, Sophia never had figured out exactly how to talk to Jessica. "I was just—quoting from a musical," she said quickly, feeling that she owed Jessica an explanation. "*Guys and Dolls*."

"Oh, *Guys and Dolls*!" Elizabeth said enthusiastically, setting down the paintbrush she was holding. "I *love* that show. Sure, I remember that line!" She pointed a finger at Sophia and narrowed her eyes. "Sky Masterson sings it: 'Mine, I leave to chance and chemistry,' and Sarah says, 'Chemistry?' and he says—"

"'Yeah, chemistry,'" Sophia finished. She smiled tentatively at "Jessica." "That's funny. I wouldn't have thought you were very interested in old Broadway shows. But I guess you learn something new every . . ." Her voice trailed off. "Are you all right?"

A sudden change seemed to have come over Jessica. Not looking at Sophia, she grabbed the paintbrush and stuck it back into the paint can. "Well, as a matter of fact," she said in a bored voice, "I don't really like shows like that. Of course, my sister, *Elizabeth*, likes that kind of thing."

"Oh." Sophia chewed nervously on a fingernail and frowned. But if Jessica wanted to be that way, Sophia guessed it wasn't *her* problem. She draped the bunting over a hook on the wall. "'Yeah, chemistry,'" she muttered softly, and hummed the rest of the song to herself.

Think next time, Elizabeth, Elizabeth commanded herself. She'd been working extra hard for the last five minutes, ever since she'd almost given herself away to Sophia. She was still kicking herself over that one. *Of course Jessica doesn't like old musicals*, she told herself sternly.

And worse than almost giving herself away, she'd had to sort of insult one of her best friends too. Elizabeth wished she could apologize to Sophia, who was hanging bunting and humming show tunes, but apologizing was just about Jessica's least favorite thing to do, and Elizabeth couldn't very well apologize as herself.

The bleachers creaked as two men, *Young Love* staffers, clambered up. "Hey, Antoine, do you know where the fuse box is?" the first man asked. Elizabeth noticed that he wore a tag that said his name was Drew.

"Basement," Antoine said, taking the wooden slats two at a time. "Why?"

Drew shrugged. "I gotta check to see if it can handle the heavy equipment."

Antoine raised his eyebrows. "You mean the fog machine?"

"Nope," Drew replied with a snort. "The other stuff. You know. For after they catch the cheaters."

Cheaters! Elizabeth got to her feet, her heart hammering. The paintbrush fell from her hand, staining the wood of the bleachers bright green, but she barely noticed. Her throat felt numb, and her body seemed as cold as ice. *Cheaters!*

But . . . how could they have found out?

"Cool," Antoine said. The two men swung over the railing at the top of the bleachers and disappeared onto a walkway. "Hey, whatever the boss says, right?"

Elizabeth willed herself to move. *Jessica*, she thought miserably. *Jessica must have spilled the beans somehow.* Her mind raced, and panic seized her heart. If they found out that she'd cheated, what would they do?

"Did he say . . . cheated?" Sophia croaked.

Elizabeth had forgotten about her friend. She whirled around. Sophia was gripping the bunting so tightly, her knuckles were turning white. *Stay calm,* Elizabeth ordered herself. *Don't show Sophia that you're upset.* She flashed Sophia her sunniest smile. *No, scratch that. Jessica wouldn't be calm, she'd be angry, right?* Quickly she changed the smile to a frown. "Cheated!" she blustered. "Who would do something dumb like that? Didn't they know they'd spoil the dance for everybody?" Her voice sounded shaky and cracked to her, but maybe Sophia wouldn't notice.

"What a bummer," Sophia said. She slid her hand along the bunting. "I c-can't imagine who would do that. C-Can you?" Elizabeth could see Sophia's knee trembling.

"N-No, I can't," Elizabeth croaked, trying to sound like her sister. She pressed her palm against her chest. "Of course, *I'm* innocent," she lied, not daring to meet Sophia's eyes.

"Oh, so am *I*," Sophia said, sounding shocked that anyone would even consider accusing her. "I'm, like, a hundred percent innocent. *Two* hundred percent."

There was silence. Elizabeth felt she should say something more. "Cheating!" she exclaimed. "And in a TV game show too! What is this world coming to?"

"They ought to be, um, tossed in jail for all eternity," Sophia said with feeling, her eyes darting anxiously left and right.

Elizabeth sighed loudly, hoping she sounded just like Jessica. "They certainly should be," she added, crossing her fingers behind her back just in case.

"Well, I—I guess I'll see you later, Jessica," Sophia stammered. She dropped the bunting, but her hands continued to flex and grip on their own. Inside she trembled like a leaf in a tornado. "I hate to run, but I just remembered I, um, have to meet somebody for lunch," she lied, seizing the first excuse that popped into her mind. She edged down the bleacher steps, her mind racing.

"Lunch?" Elizabeth stared at Sophia. Sophia noticed that "Jessica" had developed a weird tic in her right eye. "But it's only ten o'clock—"

"It takes a long time to get there by bike!" Sophia burst out. With a hasty wave, she turned and fled down the bleachers, the wooden slats sagging under her weight. *Oh, man*, she thought with a sinking feeling in her heart. *They're on to me.*

How could they possibly know? Sophia urged her feet to go faster. At the bottom of the bleachers she turned left and dashed across the gym floor. If only she could get out to the parking lot before the van left. Maybe it had had engine trouble or something. . . .

Sophia's teeth chattered, but not from cold. Picking up speed, she narrowly missed a *Young Love* staffer wheeling stereo speakers off a truck. "Hey!" he growled, but Sophia didn't miss a step. *Let it be there*, she begged silently, sprinting through the front door of the gym. *Please let the van still be there. . . .*

She ran up short.

The van was gone.

But in her mind's eye, Sophia could still see the last row. Patrick on the left. Maria in the middle. And Marshall on the right.

She knew she was right. She had to be.

Drew and Antoine had talked about the show

catching cheaters. And who better to catch cheaters than some guy who just shows up out of nowhere and goes off to the amusement park with the group?

She stared at the empty spot where the van had been, picturing Marshall in her head. There was a terrible feeling of doom in the pit of her stomach.

It all fit together. The way Marshall had hesitated when he introduced himself to her and Patrick: *"I'm a relative of Byron's,"* he'd said. *"I'm his, um, cousin,"* with that little hesitation, like he wasn't sure. Or like he was trying to remember his cover story. Just like a spy.

Dread seized Sophia. She forced herself to think straight. If Marshall was a spy, she reasoned, then it made sense for him to try to get close to Maria. He'd sit with Maria and Patrick—spend the whole day with them, maybe. He'd pretend he was interested in Maria, but he'd really be watching Maria and Patrick the whole time. "Chemistry," she repeated under her breath. Nervously she lifted her hand and rubbed her chin.

Marshall would be checking the so-called chemistry between Maria and Patrick. And it wouldn't take him long to realize that it was fake. Then he'd probably whip out his sheriff's badge and his light saber or whatever FBI guys carried and say, "Ok, what's the real story here?" She shut her eyes, feeling dizzy.

She hoped she could find a good lawyer.

But first, she realized, there was one chance. If she could catch up to Patrick and tell him to pay more attention to Maria, then maybe they could still fool the spy.

Maybe.

It's worth a try, a little voice inside her head whispered.

Sophia nodded. Yes, it was definitely worth a try. And if she was lucky, she wouldn't be too late.

Opening her eyes, she dashed for the nearest bus stop.

Four

"I'm really glad I met you," Maria said sincerely. She smiled at Marshall, who smiled back. "I don't usually meet people who like old movies as much as I do."

Marshall's eyes sparkled. "Well, when you've spent your entire life watching the Incredibly Late Show every chance you get . . ." His voice trailed off.

The van turned a sharp corner. Maria felt her body slide gently toward Marshall's tall frame. For an instant she was resting against his shoulder. "Your parents let you stay up to watch it?" she asked curiously as the van turned the other way.

"Well, there *is* school and stuff," Marshall said, his cheeks turning slightly red. "But with an—I mean, a *cousin* in show business, my folks are pretty good about that kind of thing. Especially during the summertime." He shrugged, and his hand jostled Maria's.

"Hey. Did you ever see that romantic comedy *Gardiner Expressway*? With Caroline Duran?"

"I've never even heard of it," Patrick put in from the other side of Maria. "*Gardiner Expressway*?" Maria could scarcely believe her ears. Ignoring Patrick, she leaned close to Marshall. "That's the funniest film of all time! I can't believe you know it! I love that scene where they're in the schoolhouse, about to get married, and it turns out that the best man forgot the marriage license." Maria could see the movie in her head just as clearly as if she'd seen it yesterday.

"This is *so* cool!" Marshall gave Maria a lopsided grin. "I think you're the only person I've ever met who's seen it. Even *Byron* hasn't seen it."

Maria felt her heart beating faster. So Marshall wasn't just a film buff, but a fan of romantic comedies—and of *Gardiner Expressway*, the best romantic comedy of all time. "And you know what?" she asked, barely touching the sleeve of Marshall's shirt. "I actually *worked* with Caroline Duran once."

"No *way!*" Marshall turned to stare at Maria, mouth wide open.

"Why haven't I heard of her?" Patrick wondered aloud.

"She was kind of old by then," Maria said, remembering, "but she was so sweet. She actually talked to me, and not all the actors would."

The van lurched across a pothole. This time Marshall was flung practically into Maria's lap.

She laughed. No doubt about it, she was definitely developing a crush on Marshall.

"What did she talk about?" Marshall raised his eyebrows. "About moviemaking, agents, things like that?"

Maria shook her head. "About her life. How she had gotten chicken pox on a ship from England to the United States once, and how she had a pet turtle named Smedley, and . . . oh, stuff like that." She smiled at Marshall. "She's one of my favorites, though, that's for sure."

"I think they should have given her an Academy Award for that movie," Marshall said, nodding. "Here's another one of hers. Ever see *My Canadian Friend*? With, you know, that actor from Chile and—"

"Oh, *yes!*" Maria burst out, unable to contain her enthusiasm. She grinned at Marshall and shifted position so she'd be closer to him.

First *Gardiner Expressway* and now *My Canadian Friend*. Two of the greatest, least-known movies ever made. And Marshall knew and loved them both.

Some things were just meant to be, she decided, lifting her head to see him a little better.

They were talking about me and Jessica, Elizabeth told herself, fighting back a sense of panic. She stood outside the gym, wondering what she should do. With Sophia gone, she wasn't pretending to be Jessica anymore.

Cheaters. That was what Drew had said. *Cheaters.* There wouldn't be any dance that night, and it was her fault. Hers and Jessica's. Well, mostly hers, because it had been her idea. Jessica must have gotten tired of being around Todd and let something slip.

A chill crept up from the base of Elizabeth's spine. What would they do to her if they found out the truth?

Her mind focused on her sister, who was on the van somewhere between the school and Dizzy Planet. With Todd. Either being obnoxious to him, or else standing up and proclaiming to the entire van—including Byron Miller himself—that she was a fake. Both possibilities seemed pretty awful. One way, Elizabeth suspected, she'd lose her sort-of boyfriend. The other way, she'd mess up the dance for everyone at school.

Not to mention that they might get into some serious trouble.

Elizabeth took a deep breath and tried to calm her foot, which was bouncing up and down on the pavement. There was only one chance. If she hustled on down to the bus stop, she might be able to hop on an express, which would drop her off at Dizzy Planet. Then she could buy a ticket, go on in, and find Jessica. She'd explain the situation to her sister—if it wasn't already too late—and take her place.

Which would make the game honest.

And keep Todd from thinking that she didn't really like him.

A metallic groan jarred Elizabeth from her thoughts. She stared, dismayed, as a large bus trundled by, smoke belching from the tailpipe. *My bus*, she thought with a sinking feeling. Quickly she checked the sign. *Number six express. Darn, darn, darn.*

She raised her hand to signal the driver, but the bus continued on. As it drove away, Elizabeth caught sight of a familiar-looking figure in the back window. Elizabeth blinked. It looked almost like Sophia.

But what would Sophia be doing on a bus when she was riding her bike to a lunch date?

Well, there was no time to think about that now. Shaking her head, Elizabeth broke into a jog. The bus stop was only a short distance away, but she wasn't about to take the chance of missing the next one too.

"Ms. Sylvester sure can't drive," Todd said faintly to Jessica. He leaned back in his seat as the van screeched to a sudden stop at a red light. "Hasn't she ever heard of the brake?"

"Ms. Sylvester doesn't believe in brakes," Byron said from the other side of Jessica. "She drives in two gears: reverse and warp speed. Anyway, you want to get to Dizzy Planet soon, don't you?"

"Um . . ." Todd put a hand over his stomach.

Jessica peered at Todd. No doubt about it, he was looking a little bit green. Hope leaped inside her. If Todd got carsick this easily, he probably would want to stick with the baby rides at Dizzy Planet. The Twenty-Three-Degree Tilt and the Antigravity Galaxy wouldn't be good for his stomach. Which meant that if she insisted they go on those rides, she might be able to sneak away and lose him. Maybe even go on a few rides with Janet, if *she* could manage to lose

Donald. In front of her she could see Janet, arms folded and lips pursed, staring straight ahead while Donald tried to make conversation.

Yeah, Jessica thought, nodding to herself. Things were looking up.

"So how's the show doing in the ratings?" she ventured, leaning across toward Byron. Maybe she could even go on some rides with him. Hey, as long as she came back with Todd, everything was OK, right?

"Oh, you know." Byron waved his hand in the air. "Even a great show like this doesn't last forever. Got to have a few other irons in the fire."

"Oh." Jessica wasn't sure she understood. "You mean, like, you have another project you're thinking about?" It was strange to think of Byron Miller doing any show but *Young Love*.

Byron laughed. "My lips are sealed," he said in a silky voice. "Let's just say that there's more to life than *Young Love*."

The light changed to green. The van moved forward with a nauseating lurch, picked up speed, and switched lanes without warning. Jessica swallowed hard.

Todd moaned. "I sure hope there aren't any more lights between here and the park," he commented.

Jessica frowned. A thought struck her. It wasn't the nicest thing in the world to do to Todd, but . . . "Say, Todd?" she asked, fluttering her eyelashes at him. She motioned to a Dizzy Planet brochure on the seat beside him. "I was wondering if you could look up a couple of things for me about the park."

Todd grinned weakly. "Sure, Elizabeth," he murmured. "I'd—love to."

"Oh, good!" Jessica said. Reading always made her own carsickness worse, so probably it would do the same thing for Todd. If he got sick, then she'd be able to spend the day with Byron. She stole a quick glance at him. Boy, was he cute. And he had a nice personality too. . . .

Todd opened the brochure and stared at it for a few seconds. He breathed deeply. "Um—what do you want to know?"

Jessica considered. "How large is the park?"

"I can answer that question!" Byron flashed Jessica a brilliant smile. Reaching into a briefcase, he pulled out a slim paperback with a photo of the Antigravity Galaxy ride on the cover. "Much better than that brochure," he confided, flipping the book open. "This one tells you everything. I got it since I'm in the media." He ran his finger down a page. "Let's see . . . number of cotton candies sold per hour, no . . . maximum velocity of roller coaster, no . . . target demographics, whatever *that* means—"

"Um," Todd broke in, turning toward Byron, "she asked *me*."

"No problem, my man!" Byron turned another two pages. "It's just that *my* book is to *your* book as the Antigravity Galaxy is to a merry-go-round. Might as well go with the best." His eyes narrowed. "Size of park. Here we go."

Jessica grasped Byron's sleeve. She would much rather listen to Byron, but right now she was trying to get Todd sick—and Byron wasn't helping. "Um, Byron?" she began.

"One tenth the size of the state of Rhode Island," Byron announced cheerfully. "Half again as big as, um, O'Hare International Airport. In Chicago. You ever been there? That's *some* airport. You could practically walk through the terminal for three days and never get to the other end." He whistled appreciatively. "Hey! And listen to this! There are more miles of moving sidewalk at Dizzy Planet than in New York City, Houston, and Minneapolis combined!"

The van made a sharp left, then a sudden swerving right. Jessica fell into Byron's lap. Todd groaned louder. "Byron—" Jessica began.

"Cool!" Byron paid no attention. "Know why they call the Ferris wheel the Ferris wheel? You'll never guess. Because it was named after some guy called Ferris, that's why. George Ferris. He built the first one back in Chicago a hundred years ago." He held the book closer to his face. "But this doesn't say if it was at O'Hare Airport."

Brakes screeched. Ms. Sylvester brought the van to a stop inches behind a police cruiser. Jessica could feel her stomach continue on a few more feet ahead of her body. Her hips bounced up against the seat belt. "Really, Byron," she tried again. "That's all cool and everything, but I think Todd—"

"No, it's all right." Todd's voice sounded froggy. "I

think I'll . . . just . . . take a little nap." He managed a wan grin. "If it's, you know, OK with you, I mean."

"Well . . . um . . . ," Jessica began.

"Cool," Byron said quickly. He brought the guidebook closer to his face as Ms. Sylvester hit the gas pedal. The van accelerated through the intersection. "Let's see, what else? Did you hear about this dude named—hang on . . ." Jessica could see him squinting. "Named, um, Planet. His first name was Davey, no, Dizzy. . . . Oops, scratch that, he wasn't a guy at all, he was the amusement park." Byron smiled at Jessica. "Sorry about that. I was going to say, did they name the park after him or was it the other way around?"

Jessica sighed.

"Oh, and listen to this!" Byron burst out. "This says that they built Dizzy Planet at a cost of only a million dollars . . . I mean billion . . . wait a minute . . ." A frown creased his forehead. "How many zeroes is that, anyway?" Holding the book this way and that, he stared at the page while the van rumbled forward. "Nine . . . no, ten . . . no . . ."

"Probably a billion," Jessica said. She craned her neck. In the distance she could see the high roller coaster that was the trademark of Dizzy Planet.

"Eleven—no, that's a speck. . . ." Byron blinked twice, rubbed his eyes, and stared harder at the page in front of him. Then he breathed deeply and swallowed.

"Are you all right?" Jessica turned to look at him, concerned.

"Um—" Byron swallowed again and grinned, but

not as widely as he had earlier. "That is to say—I—" He coughed, and Jessica noticed how pale he suddenly looked. "I'm sorry, Elizabeth. I guess I probably shouldn't have . . . read . . . from the book." He wiped beads of perspiration off his forehead. "I think I'll go lie down next to the air-conditioning vent." Moving slowly, he stood and threw his long body down on an empty seat.

Jessica scowled. Well, Todd felt sick, all right. But now Byron did too.

Bummer.

"Dizzy Planet!" Ms. Sylvester boomed out, pulling to an abrupt stop in the parking lot. "All ashore who're going ashore!"

Maria looked around, startled. Were they there already? She unbuckled her seat belt and stood up. "I guess time flies when you're having fun!" she said brightly, grinning at Marshall.

"I guess so!" Marshall stepped into the aisle and bowed extravagantly. "After you, ma'am."

"Thank you, sir," Maria said, dropping him a deep curtsy. She walked past him and climbed out of the van.

Once outside, Maria smiled at Patrick, and they started walking toward the gates to the park. Marshall seemed to hang back.

Maria looked over her shoulder. "Aren't you coming?" she asked Marshall.

Marshall colored slightly. "I suppose . . ." His voice

trailed off, and he shifted uncomfortably from one foot to the other. "I mean, technically, you're really going to the park with this guy here." He nodded at Patrick.

Patrick. Maria bit her lip. *That's right.* She and Patrick were supposed to sort of be on a date. Suddenly that seemed really strange. "Well . . . ," she said slowly, not wanting to hurt Patrick's feelings, but wanting also to find some way to see more of Marshall.

"Oh, well, hey," Patrick said with a shrug. "You guys are getting along so well, it's no skin off my nose if you hang out with us, Marshall." He grinned feebly. "As long as you promise to talk about something besides movies once in a while, OK?"

"Oh, Patrick." Maria's heart leaped. What an understanding, *sensitive* guy. This was just perfect. She touched his shoulder. "That's so sweet of you."

"Hey." Patrick looked embarrassed. "No big deal."

"Of course not," Maria said warmly. She couldn't believe her good luck.

"Great." Marshall's eyes shone. "That way, you guys stick to the rules. Just in case they've got, you know, *spies* watching." His eyes twinkled.

Patrick looked curiously at Byron, who was stretched across the seat in front of them, groaning. "What's wrong with the boss?" he asked.

Ms. Sylvester sat up straight and glared menacingly at Patrick. "He's carsick," she snapped. "And would you believe he blames *my* driving?"

Five

◇

"All right, guys, how about the game room?" Todd asked. He smiled weakly at Jessica. "I don't think I'm ready for anything more than that yet. If you know what I mean."

Jessica couldn't help making a face. She knew, all right. Her trick had backfired. Todd was getting the color back in his face, while Byron was stretched out in the van with his mouth practically attached to the air-conditioning vent.

Still, she was at Dizzy Planet, at last. And it was one great place, that was for sure. She stared off into the distance, at the twin peaks of the roller coaster and the low hill of the Monster Splash. Was that the Antigravity Galaxy over to the right? She shut her eyes, listening to the little kids yelling excitedly, smelling the cotton candy and buttery popcorn.

"The game room." Aaron nodded enthusiastically. "Where they have all those booths where you pop balloons with darts and stuff like that?"

Todd grinned. "Yeah. Only it's a little more high-tech here at Dizzy Planet—we'll probably have to pop balloons with laser beams or something."

A smile curved onto Aaron's lips. "I could go for that," he said. "In fact—" His eyes sparkled. "Amy, I challenge you to a contest. You're always talking about what a great athlete you are. Why don't you prove it? I bet you can't beat me at a single one of these games."

"Oh, I could too." Amy tossed her hair out of her face and glared at Aaron, annoyed. "I could clobber you at *any* game you can think of."

"Could not." Aaron shrugged casually and sketched a line in the dirt with his foot. "Of course, if you're so sure you'll lose . . ." The challenge hung in the air.

"Lose!" Amy scoffed. "Forget about it, Aaron. I'll take your challenge, and I'll blow you out of the water too!"

Todd laughed. "Elizabeth and I don't have to make a bet, do we, Elizabeth? But I'll win you a teddy bear."

Jessica smiled brightly, wishing that Todd would win her Byron instead. "How nice, Todd," she murmured. Actually, a competition sounded pretty decent. It would be interesting, and anyway, she was pretty sure she could win against Todd.

"Know what I'd like to see?" Janet asked. "A

competition between Donald Nerdling here and a worm. I bet the worm would whip him. Especially at anything that needs hands."

Jessica was about to laugh, but then remembered that she was supposed to be her sister. "That wasn't nice, Janet," she scolded.

Donald stepped forward suddenly, his jaw set and a determined look on his face. "Thanks, Elizabeth," he said in a brittle voice. "But I'll handle this myself." He turned to face Janet. "I'm sick of you calling me a nerd," he said loudly. "I didn't come here to be insulted."

"Is that right?" Janet asked nastily. "Then what did you come here for?" She gave him a mocking half smile.

But Donald pushed on. "I came here to, um, challenge you to a competition," he said, his voice louder than before. "I bet I can beat you at any game you choose in there." He stuck out his hand. "Deal?"

Janet snickered. "He's challenging *me?*" she asked, rolling her eyes. "As *if* he could possibly win. It would be like the Lakers playing against a team of frogs."

Donald swallowed hard. "I'm challenging you," he said, his voice rising in pitch. "Are you chicken or what?"

"Excuse me?" Janet spun around quickly and glared down at Donald. "What did you call me?"

Donald held his ground. "I challenged you to a competition," he repeated. "Unless you're too *chicken* to take it. Bock, bock, bo-ock!"

Jessica raised her eyebrows. She was actually kind of impressed that Donald would stand up to Janet. Not too many people had that much courage.

"Aw, c'mon, Janet," Aaron said idly. "Take the stupid bet."

"You're not chicken for real, are you?" Todd cocked his head to the side.

"Oh, for heaven's sake." Janet puffed out her cheeks. "All right. Let the little nerd have his way." Gingerly she took Donald's outstretched hand and shook it. "We'll have a games contest, and I'll win," she added confidently, dropping Donald's hand and wiping her own on her jeans.

Todd grabbed for Jessica's arm. "Let's go," he murmured. "I think they've got one of those miniature bowling games over here. Teddy bear, here we come!"

Jessica wrinkled her nose. *A contest would be much more fun,* she thought gloomily. "You know, Todd," she ventured, "I was thinking that a contest might be kind of interesting." She glanced at his face to see how he would react. "Just a friendly little bet between the two of us."

"Well, OK." Todd knit his brow. "But I really want to win you a teddy bear first."

He looked so earnest that Jessica decided she'd better backtrack. "Well, I didn't really mean it," she said, swallowing her disappointment and looking longingly after Amy and Aaron.

With a sigh she allowed Todd to steer her toward the game room door.

*   *   *

Oh, man. Oh, man. Sophia stood uncertainly at the entrance to Dizzy Planet, her head feeling as dizzy as the amusement park rides. In front of her was a long line of people buying tickets. Tickets to get into the park.

And she had . . . Her fingers groped in her purse. Two dollars . . . three . . . was that a five-dollar bill? No, of course not, it was only another single. Plus a few quarters and a dime and a couple of nickels.

That was it. She shook her head sadly. Less than five dollars, once you subtracted bus fare home.

And admission was going to cost her *way* more than five dollars. Way, *way* more. Sophia stared up at the two humps of the roller coaster. Twenty dollars? Twenty-five? *Thirty*-five? She wet her lips, wondering what to do. One thing was for sure: She didn't have that kind of money.

Just go home, a little voice inside her head urged her.

And let Marshall, the spy intent on catching the cheaters, figure out the whole thing? another voice argued. In her mind's eye she could see Marshall hanging around Patrick and Maria somewhere in the park, seeing that they didn't have any chemistry between them and blowing the whistle.

No. She had to get in.

Somehow.

"The Ferris wheel's my favorite," Marshall said, grinning his lopsided grin.

"Really?" Maria raised her eyebrows. She grinned back. "What a coincidence. Mine too."

It's not such a big deal, she told herself. So Marshall loved the same movies she did. And he was kind of cute and a good conversationalist. And now it turned out that they had the same taste in amusement park rides.

Well, that didn't mean they were destined for each other.

Although she had to admit, it was weird.

Patrick shrugged. "The Ferris wheel's OK," he said indifferently. "Whatever. I hear Dizzy Planet's got a really cool video arcade." His eyes lit up. "With all the cutting-edge games. Ever played Sand Blasters Three?"

"Um, no," Marshall replied. Then he gestured toward the Ferris wheel and caught Maria's eye. "Shall we?"

"We shall!" Maria said enthusiastically.

Riding the Ferris wheel with Marshall. She could feel butterflies in her stomach.

What a *romantic* suggestion.

Sophia noticed a line of little kids standing near the ticket booth. A large woman and a few teenagers were with them. *A group from a day care center or something,* she decided. Swallowing hard, she edged over to the group. Maybe she could just "happen to" join it.

"Tiny Tots Play Care!" a man's voice shouted. Sophia jerked her head up to see a red-faced, balding man holding up a handful of brightly colored tickets. He motioned toward the children. "Time to go on in, kiddies!"

Kiddies. Sophia made a face. She hated it when grown-ups used silly words like that. She stepped closer to the line. Did she really dare?

Did she really have a choice?

"Counselors, find your kids!" the man bellowed. Sophia watched as the teenagers went to find places in the line. Now was her chance. Maybe they wouldn't count heads very carefully. Maybe they wouldn't know she wasn't working for them. . . .

Maybe they'd put her in jail for the rest of her life for cheating Dizzy Planet out of the admission fee.

Well, she was already in pretty big trouble, she reminded herself. And it was now or never. Pretending she belonged, she went to stand next to a runny-nosed little girl in a Tiny Tots Play Care T-shirt and a pair of shorts with a smiling panda sewn to the seat.

"Hi, honey," she said, taking the little girl's hand. "My name's Sophia."

"Hi, Thophia," the girl said thickly, wiping her nose on Sophia's wrist.

Ugh, gross, Sophia thought, suppressing a shudder. The line started moving forward slowly. Sophia could feel her heart pounding in her chest. *I can't believe I'm doing this,* she thought.

"Will you put me on the thwing, Thophia?" the little girl asked.

"On the what?" Sophia took a deep breath.

Ahead of her, kids and counselors trooped through a heavy gate. A young man watched, looking bored, as one person after another pushed the lever that made the low gate slide open. *It's probably just an act*, Sophia told herself, terrified. *He's pretending he isn't really looking, but when I go through he'll pounce on me and say, "Where's your ticket?" and—*

"The *thwing*," the girl repeated.

"Oh, the *thwing*," Sophia said. Two people to go. One. "Sure, sweetie. I'll push you on the thwing just as soon as—" She gulped and stepped forward, grabbing the gate lever with her free hand. *This is it*, she told herself hollowly. Sophia willed the young man to keep his eyes focused anywhere but on her.

"And the *thlide*," the girl said with a pout. "I like to go down the thlide too. Will you take me?"

"Of courth I will." Sophia tugged at the lever, but it wouldn't budge. Fear coursed through her body. *They know*, she told herself, pulling harder. *They've got this rigged somehow so I can't get in.* Sweat dripped off her body. Biting her lip, she yanked with all her strength—

"Hey, you!"

Trembling, Sophia stood up straight. *Oh, no*, she thought hollowly, turning to face the young man. She opened her mouth to confess everything, but he interrupted before she could say a word.

"You *push*," he said, demonstrating with his hand. "Don't *pull*." Under his breath he muttered something that sounded like "stupid idiot."

But Sophia was too relieved to care. "Um— thanks," she said, giving the lever a gentle push. The gate slid open. Sophia stepped through.

She drew a deep breath.

She was in!

"What do you think of roller coasters?" Maria asked timidly as she, Marshall, and Patrick made their way toward the Ferris wheel.

Marshall laughed and ran his hand through his hair. "I like 'em! Maybe not as much as Ferris wheels, but they're pretty cool too. Especially when they go upside down." He turned his palm so it faced the sky. "Vroom! Like that!"

Maria grinned. It was so cool, the way she and Marshall had all these likes and dislikes in common. "Me too," she said. "How do you feel about, um, merry-go-rounds?"

Patrick groaned. "Oh, *please*," he said.

"Promise not to tell anybody?" Marshall smiled impishly. "I *love* merry-go-rounds. Especially if they have elephants and tigers to ride on. Or those teacup thingies that spin."

"Same here!" Maria gasped. How many guys her age would admit to liking merry-go-rounds? she wondered. Two? Three? "Maybe we could go for a merry-go-round ride later on," she said shyly. "If the one here is any good, that is."

"Count me out," Patrick said from behind them. "I'll be looking for the video games. Sand Blasters

Three won a Critic's Choice Award when they reviewed it in—" He broke off suddenly.

Maria frowned. "What's up?' she asked.

Patrick pointed to a neon sign, a huge grin on his face. "Video Arcade," he read excitedly. He slapped the tokens in his pocket. "Um, if you two don't mind," he said quickly, "I'll skip the Ferris wheel." He turned toward the sign, but then hesitated. "That *is* OK, isn't it?" he asked, sounding worried. "You guys have a ton in common anyway. You don't mind, right?"

Mind? Maria swung back to look at Marshall, and her heart stirred. A Ferris wheel ride with Marshall, all alone. Did she *mind?*

That was an easy one.

"No problem!" she said cheerfully.

"Only a hundred and sixty-five this time," Todd said with a sigh. He fished in his pocket for another token. "The machine must be all messed up or something. Sorry, Elizabeth. I guess I'll try again."

Jessica couldn't help a yawn. Watching Todd play the miniature bowling game was incredibly boring. Especially because he wasn't any good at it. He'd already gone through more than half the tokens the *Young Love* people had given him for the day, and he'd won exactly twenty-eight tickets so far.

She lifted her eyes toward the smallest teddy bear behind the counter. A tag next to it said it cost a hundred tickets. "Seventy-two to go," she mumbled under her breath.

Todd dropped a token into the slot and pulled the lever. Two wooden balls tumbled down the gutter toward him, and ten miniature pins sprang into place. Todd blew on his hands, grasped the first ball firmly, and rolled it toward the pins.

The ball spun left, struck one pin, and disappeared into the gutter.

"I can't believe it!" Todd said. "Well, maybe I can pick up the spare." Seizing the second ball, he rolled it after the first. This time he knocked down two pins.

"Three," Jessica said, trying to keep the boredom out of her voice.

Todd shook his head. "Something's got to be wrong with the game," he said with conviction. "Usually I get, like, ten strikes in a row." He peered at the next ball, which had just come rolling down the chute. "Maybe the balls aren't completely round or something. Hey, yeah. I bet that's it. What do you think, Elizabeth?"

I think I'm not about to waste my whole day here watching you, Jessica thought, but all she said was, "Maybe you're right."

Six

◇

"Patrick!"

Out of breath, Sophia flung herself across Patrick's video game. Three blue creatures with laser guns flickered on the screen and disappeared.

"Sophia!" Patrick stood back, took off his helmet with the 3-D visor, and glared at her. "Hey, what's the big idea? You messed me up just when I was about to break six billion points!" Then his expression shifted from angry to confused. "And what are you doing here?"

Sophia wanted to explain, but there was no time. "Listen," she hissed, sure that some agent from the Secret Service was hot on her trail. "Where are Maria and Marshall?" It was lucky that Dizzy Planet had a video arcade. Knowing Patrick, she'd guessed right away where to find him.

"Maria and Marshall?" Patrick looked exasperated. "Is that all? You come here and jostle my arm and cover the screen so I can't see where the motorized jellyfish are hiding, and—"

Sophia bit her lip. Why couldn't Patrick understand how important this was? "Listen, Patrick," she said as he groped in his pocket for another token, "this is *serious*. Don't you know who Marshall *is?*"

"He's Byron's cousin," Patrick snapped. "Now if you'll—"

"But he *isn't*," Sophia said desperately, hanging on to his sleeve. "He's an *impostor*. He's a spy, and he's trying to prove that we cheated, and if you don't go right back to Maria and try to at least pretend that you're interested in her, he's going to figure out the truth!" She realized she was yelling and clamped her mouth shut. "I mean it, Patrick," she whispered.

All at once Patrick looked shaken. "A . . . spy?" he whispered, his eyes darting left and right.

Sophia was afraid to speak, but she nodded slowly.

"Oh, man." Patrick chewed on his lower lip. "A spy. You know, he said something about spies, but I didn't really think about it. How we had to stay together just in case there might be spies—" He broke off.

Sophia felt her blood running cold. "He was giving you a *hint*," she said numbly. "Like, a fair chance. If you'd figured it out, you'd have stuck with Maria and . . ." She took a deep breath. "Patrick, you've got to go find them," she said, grabbing his hand and pressing it tightly between hers. "Make sure Marshall doesn't get suspicious. Do whatever it takes."

Patrick stared at her, his mouth a tight line. "Whatever it takes," he repeated. "I guess I'd better. Last time I saw them, they were heading toward the Ferris wheel." He looked from Sophia to the video game and back. "If only—"

"If only what?" Sophia prompted.

Patrick took one last glance toward the Sand Blasters Three machine. "Well, if you could, like, keep the machine warm for me while I'm gone, that would be great," he said, coloring slightly. "I'm on a roll here and—"

Sophia squeezed her eyes shut and gave Patrick a push. "Just *go!*" she whispered frantically.

And when she opened her eyes again, Patrick was gone.

Money. Elizabeth stood at Dizzy Planet's ticket counter, trying not to panic. The signs didn't even bother to say how much it cost to get in, which was bad news right there. *If you have to ask, you can't afford it.*

Now, if she'd been a grown-up, she could have just flashed a credit card and walked in. But no. She was only a kid, and she didn't have the seventy-five bucks or whatever it would take to get into the place.

Only, of course, she *had* to get in. It was critical for the school dance, not to mention her relationship with her sort-of boyfriend. She glanced around, wondering if there was some way she could sneak in without anybody noticing.

But there wasn't. Or if there was, she wasn't smart enough to see it.

Pretend to be a worker? she wondered, shifting from one foot to the other. But the workers had uniforms. *Sneak in with a family—a large family?* But how many families were so large that they wouldn't notice an extra daughter?

What else?

"Hey, Elizabeth!"

Startled, Elizabeth whirled around. Who had recognized her?

"Over here!" Just ahead of her, a boy waved and flashed her a brilliant smile. Her heart lurched as she recognized Byron Miller himself. "Um—hi," she called out weakly, wondering what in the world to do.

Byron obviously thought she was Elizabeth.

And although she *was* Elizabeth, she wasn't *supposed* to be Elizabeth. Because Elizabeth was supposed to be in the theme park right now with Todd. *Which means . . .*

"Hey, thanks for waiting for me!" Byron said jauntily. "What did you do with your *Young Love* T-shirt?"

He'll see the JW *monogram,* Elizabeth realized, remembering that she'd worn her twin's shirt that morning. Casually she draped one hand across the initials. She wasn't quite sure she understood what was happening, but it seemed important not to be Jessica all of a sudden. "Well, um," she said blankly. "I mean, that is—it got kind of wet. You know," she added, a glimmer of an idea coming to her. "I spilled some soda on it."

"Poor kid," Byron said. "Let's get you a new one.

Ms. Sylvester's got a whole box of them in the van." His eyes darted toward the *Young Love* van, which was gathering a large crowd in the nearby parking lot. "*If* she hasn't given them all away already. Then we'll go into the park. And *then* we'll find your dream date."

"Great!" Elizabeth exclaimed as they headed toward the van.

Maria clambered into the swaying gondola of the Ferris wheel. She'd forgotten how much she liked them. Up and up and up, all the way to the top, and then you'd hang suspended for a fraction of a second like you were standing on the top of the world—and you could see across the whole amusement park. "I love the way people look like ants from up there," she said.

Marshall seated himself beside her. "I know what you mean," he said. "It's fun to look at them. But it's also fun to look at other things."

Maria wondered what he meant by that. The attendant had seated them alone in the gondola. "It'll be, um, nice and private in the air," she ventured.

"It, er, sure will." Marshall leaned forward and grabbed the safety bar tightly.

Maria's heart sped up. She felt shy suddenly.

"Whoops! One more!" The attendant's voice cut through her thoughts. Surprised, Maria looked up to see Patrick, panting hard, diving into their gondola and scrambling between her and Marshall.

"Hi, guys!" he panted. "Hope you don't mind. I missed you!"

"Already?" Marshall asked doubtfully, but he slid over to make room.

Maria wrinkled her nose, a little disappointed. "I thought you were playing video games."

"I was," Patrick said, grinning at her. "But it got boring." He sat up straight and tucked an arm behind each of them. "There now, aren't we cozy!" he said in a more normal voice, smiling at Maria.

Maria smiled back. She didn't mind that he'd rejoined them, even though she'd really been looking forward to a little time alone with Marshall.

Patrick leaned close to her ear. "Don't tell our friend here," he whispered. "But the real reason I'm back is *you*."

Me? Maria frowned. "Um—thanks," she whispered back, confused by his sudden change in attitude. "But you really didn't have to—"

"Oh, sure I did." Patrick's voice was low, and Maria could see his eyes anxiously scanning the horizon. "I just, you know, couldn't stand to miss a chance to spend the day with you, that's all!"

Maria stared at him closely. "That's . . . sweet," she murmured, although really she thought it was strange.

She pressed her lips together, thinking hard. Then a thought struck her. Patrick was probably just feeling embarrassed because after picking her to be his partner, he'd felt like he was abandoning her. *Yeah, that must be it.* Patrick was worrying about hurting Maria's feelings. She nodded. Sure. It all fit. He'd gone and left her, which wasn't all that gentlemanly when you came right down to it, and he'd had an attack of conscience.

She smiled. "Thanks for coming back, Patrick," she said sincerely.

What a great guy!

"A seven-ten split!" Todd stared, dismayed, at the two pins still standing in front of him. "I can't believe my rotten luck!"

Some would call it rotten skill, Jessica thought. She'd never seen anyone bowl as badly as Todd. "How many tickets do you have now?" she asked, not even bothering to keep the boredom out of her voice.

"Fifty-eight." Todd sighed. "Fifty-nine if I get one of these pins on my last roll. Um—do you have any tokens left?"

It's not like I've had the chance to spend any, Jessica thought, irritated. "Listen, Todd," she said, smiling sweetly, "I don't really care all that much about a teddy bear, OK? Let's go ride the Monster Splash." She itched to leave. By now Byron might be feeling better and—

"Not *yet,*" Todd said brightly. "I really, really want to win you a bear." He rolled the last ball—and groaned as it missed the left-hand pin by a hair. "Bummer."

Jessica made a face. This was worse than boring. This was positively deadly. *And if you think this is bad, just wait until tonight!* she thought. Jessica could just imagine it—Todd would be grinning at her while she looked at Aaron, who would be in a fight with Amy, while Janet was quietly trying to murder Donald by the punch bowl. But she would deal with that later; it didn't change her current problem. She glanced around the room for some other game where Todd might do a little bit better. Shooting ray guns at aliens . . . firing a squirt gun to make moons orbit around a bright green planet . . . *aha*.

Jessica's eyes lit on a counter with a barrel sticking out of the back wall. There was a small hole in the top of the barrel. "Throw the space shuttle into the hangar," she read aloud, "and win a bear!"

"That's too hard," Todd grunted, finding a token and pulling it out.

"It might be hard," Jessica snapped back. "But it can't be any harder than this for you. Plus it'll take less time."

Todd hesitated. The token hovered above the slot. "That's true," he admitted.

Jessica saw her chance. "And after you win me the teddy bear," she went on, smiling brightly, "we can go on the Monster Splash together." She swallowed hard. "They say it's, um, nice and private."

Todd nodded slowly, and the tips of his ears turned pink. "Good idea, Elizabeth. That sounds like lots of fun. Let me just try this other game." He stepped toward the counter. "I really want to win you that bear. . . ."

Phew! Jessica wiped imaginary sweat off her brow. With any luck, maybe Todd would run out of tokens right away. Then they could—

But before she could complete her thought, she felt someone's hand close over her mouth.

"Well, that was quite a ride, huh?" Patrick beamed. He stood up and stretched, then climbed onto the Ferris wheel ramp.

"Oh, yeah," Marshall muttered, following Patrick out of the gondola. "It was great."

Maria wasn't quite sure what to say. She appreciated the attention from Patrick, but she hated to see Marshall so bummed out. And Patrick had kept up a series of compliments throughout the ride, making Maria begin to wonder just what he thought of her. It was almost beginning to feel as though he had a *crush* on her or something.

But that was crazy. Everybody knew Patrick liked Sophia.

"Hey, look at us!" Patrick called, pausing just past the exit. He jabbed his finger toward a booth where video terminals displayed pictures of the Ferris wheel riders. "Number three-sixty-two—check it out!"

Maria rolled her eyes. There were the three of them, all right—Patrick jabbering away into Maria's ear while Marshall sat frowning, his arms crossed. Not the most flattering picture she'd ever seen.

"Want to take a copy home?" an attendant asked hopefully. "The video's eight-ninety-five plus tax, and a still picture is just five dollars. Plus tax, of course. Or you can get an eight-by-ten glossy for—"

"No, thanks," Maria said, shaking her head and walking on.

Marshall stepped around Patrick and turned to Maria. "How would you like to ride the flying saucers next?" he asked.

Patrick stepped in between them. "Oh, we'd love to," he said cheerfully.

We. Maria grimaced. She stole a quick look at Marshall. "Um—yeah, that sounds like fun," she said hesitantly. "But only two can fit in a saucer at a time."

Patrick shrugged. "That's OK. I'm sure the attendant can find someone to ride with Marshall."

"Well—" Maria groped for words. "I mean—" That wasn't exactly the answer she'd been looking for, but how could she tell Patrick to buzz off—in a nice way, of course? "Or he could find another seat for—"

"You don't mind, do you, Marsh?" Patrick asked.

"Hey," Marshall said uncomfortably. "You know, nobody calls me Marsh."

Maria looked anxiously from Marshall to Patrick and back. She wished Patrick weren't being quite so persistent. And she wished Marshall weren't looking so—well, so *hurt.* But she wasn't sure what to do about it.

"Come on, Maria," Patrick said heartily, taking her arm in his.

Well, one ride won't hurt—right? Maria hoped, glancing back at Marshall as Patrick led her toward the flying saucer line.

*   *   *

"Elizabeth! You scared the living daylights out of me!"

Jessica's heart was still going a mile a minute. She stood up straight behind the electronic poker game where her twin had dragged her and glared furiously at her sister. "What business do you have barging in here and—" she began, but then she stopped herself. "Come to think of it, why are you here at all?"

"Because they know we cheated!" Elizabeth hissed. "I heard a couple of staffers talking about it. I don't know how they know, but they do. So we need to make the game honest."

"Too late for *that*," Jessica said sarcastically. She didn't like the sound of that "we." Trust Elizabeth to blame Jessica when it was all Elizabeth's fault.

Elizabeth blushed. "I know. But, um, here's what I did. Byron thought I was you . . . I mean me." She scratched her head. "I met Byron, and he doesn't know there are two of us. I got him to bring me in and then I gave him the slip."

"You what?" Jessica spread out her hands in disgust. "He's only, like, the cutest game show host in the whole univ—"

"OK, OK," Elizabeth said quickly. "But I had to lose him so I could talk to you." She grasped Jessica's hand. Jessica winced in pain. "If you go home now, right now, I can take your place and everything will be OK."

"Go *home?*" Jessica broke free of Elizabeth's grasp. "Are you out of your *mind?*" Honestly, sometimes her sister was just plain nuts. "My first and maybe only chance to spend a day at Dizzy Planet, and you want me to go home?"

"Well—" Elizabeth looked around nervously. "I guess you wouldn't have to go *home*. You could hang out here—if you kept out of our way, mine and Todd's, that is. We can't be seen together, you and I, or else it's all over."

Jessica raised her eyebrows. "You mean, you'd take Todd back? And I could do anything I wanted here?"

Elizabeth hesitated. "Yeah, I guess so. Then you could just take the city bus back to the dance and—"

"Whoa." Jessica held up her hand. Ride the smelly old bus, when she could ride in the luxury van? "No way, José. We switch back just before the trip leaves. *You* take the bus home."

"Well—" Elizabeth brushed some hair out of her eyes. "All right." She sighed heavily. "I guess. So do we have a deal?"

Jessica smiled. This was the best news she'd had all day. No more Todd. No more having to be kind old Elizabeth. Janet was still out there somewhere. And so was—her heart gave a little bounce—Byron Miller. Healthy at last.

"You're on!" she said with feeling.

"Elizabeth!"

Elizabeth came out from behind the counter and stared. Todd was running toward her, a stuffed white bear in his hands. "Where were you?" he demanded. "Look what I won!"

"Cool!" Elizabeth grinned. "What were you playing?"

"That game over there," Todd said, jerking his thumb toward a counter with a large barrel sticking out of the back wall. "Remember? It was the one you suggested I play. Actually, I kind of bounced the space shuttle by accident, and it, um, went right into the hangar."

"That's great," Elizabeth said shyly. "But wouldn't you rather have been playing the bowling game instead?"

"I did." Todd pressed the bear into Elizabeth's arms and frowned. "But I stopped. Don't you remember? You kept telling me how bored you were."

"I did?" Elizabeth swallowed hard, wondering what else her sister had said. At least Todd hadn't walked out the minute he'd seen her, so maybe there was hope. "I mean—oh, yeah, I did! Sorry," she added quickly. "I was just . . . bored. But I'm really glad you won this for me. It was so sweet of you to think of me."

Todd blinked. "Boy, you're different now," he said cheerfully. "I don't know where you just went, but it sure snapped you out of the mood you were in. No offense or anything. So, where did you say you wanted to go next?"

Elizabeth thought hard. Where had she wanted to go next?

How should *she* know?

"Oh, wherever!" she said brightly, putting her hand on Todd's elbow.

Seven

"One hot dog," Sophia said, her voice just above a whisper. "Please."

She glanced furtively over her shoulder, wishing she felt a little less jumpy. *It's going to be OK*, she told herself, taking a deep breath. Patrick would be back with Maria by now, cozying up to her and making it impossible for Marshall the spy to realize that they weren't together. *It's going to be just fine. So stop worrying already.*

Of course, Sophia knew she would have to keep out of sight until the next bus left. Way, *way* out of sight. Because if Patrick saw even the tiniest glimpse of her, he just wouldn't be able to pretend that he liked Maria anymore. No. It would be totally obvious to anyone, especially to Marshall, that Patrick had a major crush on

Sophia instead. And then they'd be toast.

Sophia bit her lip nervously. Unfortunately, the next bus back to Sweet Valley wouldn't leave for another hour.

"That'll be two-fifty," the elderly man behind the counter interrupted, handing her a huge bun with the tiniest hot dog Sophia had ever seen. "Want any toppings? They're fifty cents apiece."

Two-fifty! Sophia dug into her pocket for the one-dollar bills. "Two-fifty for *this?*" she complained.

The man chuckled. "You think that's bad, you ought to see what we charge for a soda," he said, winking at Sophia.

"I—I think I'll pass on the soda," Sophia choked out. Her heart thumped. Take two-fifty away from what she'd had before and—

Well, she barely had enough left for bus fare, that was for sure.

"And the popcorn!" the man went on, clearly enjoying himself. "You have to take out a bank loan to buy the giant-size tub. Tastes like cardboard too."

"Um—thanks for the warning," Sophia said. She slid three folded dollar bills across the counter and waited anxiously while the clerk found the correct change. Swallowing hard, she stared down at the hot dog, realizing she'd lost her appetite.

"Uh-oh, security officers coming," the man said happily, looking over Sophia's shoulder. "Bet there's been a fight. Sometimes the teenagers slug it out over who gets to ride with who through the romantic tunnel of the Monster Splash."

"Security officers?" Half frozen with fear, Sophia whirled around. Two security guards in blue-trimmed uniforms were indeed approaching the food booth. And was it Sophia's imagination, or were they staring directly at her?

"Or maybe someone sneaked in without paying," the man went on. "That happens sometimes too. You know, they've got video cameras on top of the fences and—"

"Without paying?" Beads of sweat popped out on Sophia's forehead. She watched as one guard leaned over to say something to the other. Then the second guard nodded, and his eyes swept across the crowd.

Did he give a little flicker of recognition as he looked at Sophia?

Sophia's blood ran cold. She didn't dare wait to find out.

Dropping the hot dog on the counter, she darted off into the crowd.

"Isn't this a cool ride?" Patrick asked, laying his hand gently on Maria's.

Maria forced a smile onto her face. She and Patrick were seated in one car of the flying saucer ride. Usually she'd have loved the chance to whirl around with a guy like Patrick. But right now all she could think of was Marshall.

Poor Marshall, behind them in his own flying saucer. Who had stared sadly at them the last time they'd been in the same orbit. Maria's heart went out to him.

"I'm *so* glad you moved to Sweet Valley, Maria!" Patrick exclaimed, leaning closer. "Meeting you was, like, the best thing that ever happened to me. Well, practically, anyway," he added.

"Um—thanks." Maria took a deep breath. This wasn't going to be easy. "Listen, Patrick. I *know* you like me. And—and I like you too. But we agreed that you don't have to, like, spend the whole day with me to prove it." Was any of this making sense? "I mean," she said quickly, "if you wanted to go someplace else, like the video arcade again, it wouldn't bother me."

Patrick frowned. "But I *like* spending time with you," he said. "I really do, Maria."

"Oh." Maria wasn't sure whether to be flattered or annoyed. The flying saucer began to slow. "Um, that's nice of you." Her mind raced. Patrick wasn't taking the hint, that was for sure. "But if you really wanted to—"

"You don't understand, Maria," Patrick interrupted. They were approaching the exit ramp now. He fumbled for her hand. "I don't *want* to spend time anywhere else today. I—" He turned bright pink and broke off abruptly.

"You want to spend time with me," Maria finished for him.

The saucer rocked gently into the gate. Patrick

grinned. "Yeah," he said softly. "That's about it."

"Oh." Maria stared blankly at him. "I see." She gulped. Now it all made sense. Poor Patrick. He'd chosen her as his date, and he'd been kind of low-key and everything because he was really Sophia's sort-of boyfriend. Then they'd gotten to the park, and he'd seen how much she liked Marshall, so Patrick had tried to do the right thing, the *noble* thing, and selflessly told Maria to go spend time with Marshall.

But once Maria and Marshall had gone off together, Patrick must have discovered that he just liked Maria too much. *I must have really hurt his feelings.* Guilt stabbed at her heart.

Patrick helped Maria out of the saucer. "I guess I said too much, huh?"

"Wanna buy a souvenir of your ride?" an attendant asked in a cheerful voice, gesturing toward the video displays. "Only eight-ninety-five for the complete video. Plus tax, of course. Or you can get an eight-by-ten glossy for just seven-fifty—"

"Plus tax," Maria muttered under her breath. Shaking her head, she looked at the video picture. Patrick's earnest eyes stared back at her. She felt *really* guilty now for having hurt him. It was just so *obvious* that Patrick liked her. Why hadn't she noticed it earlier? She cast a wistful glance at the picture of Marshall, just coming into the gate now in his own saucer, but she knew she couldn't risk hurting Patrick's feelings any more.

"No, Patrick," she said, laying a hand on his elbow. "I think you said just enough."

Jessica stood in the never-ending line for the Space Demon roller coaster, hoping Elizabeth and Todd wouldn't show up. She didn't really think that anyone could have found out about their switch. So as long as she stayed out of her twin's way, nothing could go wrong.

"There you are, Elizabeth!"

Jessica whirled around, forgetting that she wasn't Elizabeth any longer, and stared right into the bright eyes of Byron Miller. "Hi, Byron," she said, raising her hand to wave.

"So where'd you run off to, anyway?" Byron demanded. With an easy motion he vaulted over the rail, landing next to Jessica. "I mean, you were there one minute, and the next minute you were gone."

Jessica thought hard. She was very aware of Byron standing next to her. Very, *very* aware. "Oh, I just lost you!" she lied, smiling brilliantly. "You know how it is in crowds. But now we're together again. . . ." She let her voice trail off.

Byron laughed. "OK. For a moment I thought maybe you ran off on purpose." He sniffed the air delicately. "I mean, I *did* take a bath just last month!" he quipped.

"Run off on purpose?" Jessica tried to look as innocent as possible. "Of course not!"

Which was true, she reasoned. It was *Elizabeth* who had given Byron the slip so she could go switch places. *I didn't dump you—and I never would,* she added in her mind, stepping closer to Byron.

In fact, the more she thought about it, the more she realized that the situation was perfect. As long as she stayed out of Elizabeth's way, she could hang out with Byron all day long. "So you're going to, um, ride the roller coaster with me?" she asked, her throat suddenly dry.

I, Jessica Wakefield, practically invited the great Byron Miller on a date!

Byron leaped back as if he'd been bitten. "The *roller coaster?*" he gasped. "No, no, no, no, no, no, no! My delicate stomach can't handle the roller coaster right now, Elizabeth. Let's try something else."

Jessica drew in her breath, hoping he'd say what she thought he'd say. "Like what?" she breathed.

"Ze Monster Splash," he intoned in a vampire voice.

Yes! It was all Jessica could do not to pump her fist in the air. The Monster Splash—with Byron Miller! Her face broke out into a huge smile.

"I think that would be very nice," she said. "Let's go!"

"So, didn't you have an idea about where we should go next?" Todd said, not quite looking Elizabeth in the eye.

"I did?" Elizabeth smiled, wondering what idea Todd was talking about. They walked slowly away from the game room, where they'd just had a photo taken of themselves and the stuffed bear, all dressed up in spacesuit gear. Annie the Alien's Photo Studio, the place had called itself. It had been a little expensive, but the picture was hilarious. She clutched it tightly against the bear. "Um— when was that?"

Todd frowned. "Just before you disappeared. Remember? You said I should cut out the bowling and try that space shuttle game."

"Oh, of course," Elizabeth said quickly. "Silly me!" For good measure she hit herself on the side of the head. "Yeah, that *bowling* game," she said, hoping she wasn't saying something really dumb.

Todd nodded. "Anyway, then you said that if I stopped bowling, we could, like, go to this, um, certain place." He began to turn red. "You've got to remember, Elizabeth!"

"I remember," Elizabeth said, and bit her lower lip. What in the world had Jessica said? "That, um, certain place. Yeah! It'll be fun!" She nodded her head enthusiastically, wishing that Todd would give her a hint.

Todd smiled, but his eyes still wouldn't meet Elizabeth's. "I guess we'll be together," he said, licking his lips nervously. "*Alone* together, I mean."

Elizabeth's mind raced. Not the Space Demon, then. The flying saucers! It had to be. Each saucer had room for only two—she'd read that in some brochure or other. "Oh, yeah, we'll have lots of fun on the flying saucers," she remarked.

Todd looked crestfallen. "Not the flying saucers," he said, disappointed.

"Oh, I was just teasing," Elizabeth said quickly. "I meant the Ferris wheel." She certainly hoped it *was* the Ferris wheel.

"Elizabeth . . ." Todd's voice trailed off. "Were you just teasing me? I don't think that's very nice. When you were telling me we should go to the Monster—"

"The Monster Splash!" Elizabeth interrupted, relieved. She could feel her heart beating a little faster. Going on the Monster Splash with Todd—well! They'd get into a little boat, just the two of them, and go slowly up through the long, dark tunnel that ran up the hill, where they'd have a chance to talk and be together . . . and then scream and yell and grab each other in terror when the boat went rushing down the slide and landed right in the middle of the lake. She'd have to remember to thank Jessica for making the suggestion the next time she saw her.

Todd's face brightened. "Phew! For a minute there you had me scared! It was like you were a different person or something!"

Elizabeth couldn't help a chuckle. "No way!" she declared, pointing the way toward the Monster Splash.

"I'm the same Elizabeth Wakefield that I've always been!"

"So—do you know what you call a town where everyone has the hiccups?" Patrick asked Maria. They had left the flying saucers and were walking with Marshall toward the Space Demon.

"No, what?" Maria replied. Patrick had been cracking jokes for the last few minutes. They were fairly dumb, she thought, but she was laughing anyway so as not to hurt his feelings.

"A hick town!" Patrick elbowed Maria in the ribs. "Get it? A *hick* town?"

Maria plastered a grin on her face. "Ha, ha, ha!" she laughed, hoping it sounded sincere. "Gee, that's hilarious, Patrick. I'll have to tell all my friends."

"I don't think it's funny," Marshall commented sourly.

"Here's another," Patrick said, ignoring Marshall. "Where does the king keep his armies?"

Maria frowned, thinking. What did you call those places where soldiers slept? Barrettes—no, barracks. "In the barracks?" she guessed.

Patrick chuckled. "Nope. In his sleevies! Get it?" He held up his arm and grabbed at the sleeve. "Where does he keep his *arm*-ies?"

Maria laughed again. That one wasn't *too* bad, she had to admit.

"Tell you what. Let's do the Martian Canals

ride," Patrick said. "It's, you know, one of those rides where two people get in a boat and float down the river in a tunnel. And they have weird aliens and stuff that jump out at you." His hand closed around Maria's. "But you wouldn't have to worry, because I'd be there to protect you."

Marshall made a slight gagging noise.

"So how about it?" Patrick pressed. He jerked his thumb at Marshall. "Marsh here can wait for us at the end of the ride if he doesn't want to go solo again."

"I thought I asked you not to call me Marsh!" Marshall snapped.

Maria strained to think. Hoo boy! What a tricky situation. Patrick was so sweet, so sincere, so *nice*. And he obviously liked her a lot. And she liked him as a friend, and she'd be eternally grateful to him for picking her to be his date.

But she had to face facts. She didn't like him in *that* way. So it wasn't fair to keep leading him on.

And if she kept it up, sooner or later Marshall would go somewhere else. Which would be a shame, because Marshall was sweet too, and charming, and cute and funny and . . .

Quickly Maria came to a decision. Winking at Marshall to let him know how she still felt, she turned to Patrick.

"I'll take you up on that ride," she said. "And Marshall, I sure hope you *will* wait for us at the end."

I'll take the opportunity to let Patrick down really gently, she promised herself. It would be private inside the Martian Canals ride, and she'd be nice about it. She'd just make it really clear to him that she only liked him as a friend, nothing more. But she'd ask him to spend the rest of the day with her and Marshall, so he couldn't be too upset. And Marshall would be waiting for her at the end of the ride, and all three of them would go off together to the roller coaster and the game room and the Monster Splash, which was next door to the Martian Canals, after all—

Yes. Maria sighed deeply, savoring the idea.

She couldn't see any way it could go wrong.

Eight

◇

Sophia darted past ticket booths, ride entrances, and the game room, not daring to look back. What if the security guards were still hot on her trail? She could picture them now: rolling the hidden-camera videotape, noticing the girl with the runny nose and the "counselor" who was with her, then sending out an all-points bulletin with her photo. With a caption like "Wanted Dead or Alive: Girl Who Sneaked into the Park." *Oh, man. What if it gets into the newspapers?* Sophia wondered. Her mom would freak.

She sped through a crowd of teenagers. Her breath was coming in short gasps, her legs felt on fire. Any second now she expected to hear shouts of "Stop, thief!" or even shots fired over her head. . . .

Clutching her side, Sophia made a sharp right, following the signs for the exit.

"I can't believe it," Jessica murmured. She stepped back and sighed.

No wonder there hadn't been a line in front of the Monster Splash. A big sign in front of the entrance announced that the ride was closed for repairs. She'd been looking forward to going through it with Byron. "Bummer," she said.

"Bummer is right," Byron agreed. He patted down his perfect hair. "Well, listen, Elizabeth. There are other rides here. Like that one, for instance."

"Which one?" Jessica craned her neck.

"The Martian Canals," Byron said slowly. "Looks like a tunnel ride, only with aliens and such." He whirled to face Jessica. "I'm up for it if you are."

Jessica sighed, swallowing her disappointment. But maybe the Martian Canals ride would have boats that were only big enough for two people too.

"You bet!" she agreed.

"What a shame," Elizabeth said a few minutes later. She looked down sadly at the sign in front of the Monster Splash boarding area. A few small boats, shaped like alien sea creatures, floated silently on the still blue water. " 'Closed for repairs—sorry for the inconvenience,'" she read aloud. "Couldn't they have done the repairs at night, when nobody's here?"

Todd shrugged. "Maybe something just recently broke down."

"Maybe." Elizabeth felt terribly disappointed. She'd been looking forward to the Monster Splash. "Isn't there anything else we could ride together?" she asked. "The flying saucers or something?"

"Not the saucers." Todd shook his head. "They make me sick. But there's a ride close to here that's just for two people." Quickly he pulled the brochure out of his pocket. "The Canals of Mars, something like that. I remember noticing it earlier, when you wanted me to read out loud on the van."

"Oh . . . yeah," Elizabeth said doubtfully.

"And that ride should be right about . . . here." Todd stabbed his forefinger toward the right. "Can I read a map, or what?" he exclaimed proudly. "It's there, just down the hill a ways. So—you game?" He held out a hand to Elizabeth.

Elizabeth smiled. Well, it was disappointing not to ride the Monster Splash, but the Martian one sounded OK. And if they were lucky, the Monster Splash might be fixed before they'd have to leave.

"Let's do it!" she exclaimed.

*   *   *

Sophia stopped short and leaned against the wall of the Martian Canals, hoping her eyes were playing tricks on her.

But as she blinked and blinked again, she realized the awful truth.

It really *was* Patrick coming up the moving sidewalk toward her. Patrick and Maria, holding hands, with Marshall behind them.

Sophia knew she couldn't stay there. Marshall would figure out the truth in three seconds flat. He was a sneaky one, that was for sure. Urging her tired legs to run, she turned around—

Oh, no.

Shading her eyes in terror, Sophia held her breath. Coming in the other direction, down the hill, were Elizabeth and Byron. Byron, the host of the show, who would certainly put two and two together if he saw Sophia standing there in the amusement park. Icy fingers clutched at Sophia's heart. She couldn't go backward and she couldn't go forward. There was no escape.

Or was there?

Blood pounding through her veins, Sophia stared up at the sign over her head. Visit the Martian Canals! it screamed. Ride Through the Home of Aliens! Try It—*If You Dare!* Below the words was a fearsome-looking portrait of a green creature with piercing red eyes and a long forked tongue.

Sophia shuddered.

Which was worse, aliens or spies?

As quickly as she could, she dashed through the entrance.

"Off we go!" Todd said, smiling broadly at Elizabeth. He leaned against the low cushion at the back of the boat. "Aliens, here we come!"

"It should be fun." Elizabeth reached for his hand. So what if the ride was a little scary? She knew it wasn't real. The water was murky and looked as if it were boiling, and every now and then the boat would bang against a rock. At least the water looked shallow, Elizabeth thought—only a few inches deep. She didn't think she could have handled it if it had gone down a mile or so.

"I've been, um, thinking," Todd said in a low voice, staring into Elizabeth's eyes. He swallowed hard. "Thinking about how nice it would be to, well, to spend a day here with you, Elizabeth. Not for the rides but for the . . ." He grinned shyly. "For the romance."

"Oh, Todd." Elizabeth squeezed his hand. "That's so sweet."

"Yeah, well," Todd said softly, "you're pretty sweet too, you know. Hey—see that?" Todd pointed ahead through the dim light of the tunnel. "I bet that's going to be the first fright. The thing that looks like a snake hanging from that tree?"

"That's a pretty realistic snake," she began—and then she froze.

Seated just two boats ahead of them was Byron Miller himself.

And a girl who was unmistakably Jessica.

"I tell you, Elizabeth," Byron said cheerfully, "I'm a natural when it comes to TV. Born to act—that's me. Put a camera in front of my face and watch what happens. It's a talent."

"Um—yeah," Jessica murmured, twisting and turning in her seat. The boat chugged slowly through the Martian tunnel, but she barely noticed the movement.

Byron frowned and touched her hand. "You know, you're not acting like you're listening, Elizabeth," he commented.

"Really?" Jessica stared at him in openmouthed astonishment. But it was all an act. In fact, Jessica knew, Byron was right. She *wasn't* listening. She hadn't been listening for the last two minutes at least.

Not since she'd turned around to get a better look at an alien projected on the wall—and had seen her very own sister staring at her from two boats behind.

For the last two minutes she'd been able to think about only one thing: how to make sure Byron didn't turn around.

Because if he saw Elizabeth, the *real* Elizabeth, sitting in a boat with Todd, he'd figure everything out. And then there would be trouble. *Big* trouble.

"I'm sorry, Byron," Jessica said. "I'm just—you know, thinking about other stuff." Nervously she twirled a lock of hair around her finger. The boat plunged suddenly down a rapids chute, and Jessica gulped.

Byron grinned. "I hope you're thinking about me," he said jokingly. "So what did you think of that last computer-generated Martian, huh?" He swiveled to get a better look. "Cool the way they designed it so the knee would bend in three diff—"

"Byron!" Panic seized Jessica. She seized his sleeve before he could turn all the way around. "Look what's coming up!" she blurted, though her tongue felt as lifeless and heavy as a block of wood.

"You mean the skeleton? That's boring." Byron made a face. "All you need's a strobe effect, a good recording studio to make the special-effects noises, and a laser setup so the front of the boat trips the tape. Just a few thousand bucks is all, and hey, presto!" He snapped his fingers. "But that computer-generated one, now that's creativity for you." Hoisting himself up in the seat, he started to turn around the other way. "I bet I can tell how it—"

"Byron!" Frantic, Jessica reached up and blocked him with her body. "Um—don't leave me!" she burst out. It was the only line she could come up with on the spur of the moment.

Byron laughed easily. "Oh, Elizabeth," he said. "Don't be so—"

There was a whirring noise above their heads. A giant spider flew down from the ceiling and came to a screeching stop inches from Jessica's nose. Its eyes glowed red and it gave a fearsome hiss. An unearthly scream reverberated through the tunnel. Thinking quickly, Jessica screamed too and pretended to faint.

"Oh, man!" Byron knelt and tried to shake her awake. "Elizabeth! It's just animatronics, kid!"

"Oh, man" is right, Jessica thought, keeping her eyes firmly shut. She was disgusted with her behavior. No way was the real Jessica Wakefield terrified by dumb things like high-tech spiders.

But the real Jessica Wakefield *was* terrified of being caught.

And at least Byron wasn't looking back anymore.

"Elizabeth, it's like you haven't been listening to a word I've been saying!"

Elizabeth forced herself to take her eyes off the boat ahead and pay attention to Todd for a moment. "What did you say?" she asked as the boat bumped into a boulder and changed direction.

Todd's eyes flashed. He edged away from Elizabeth. "Elizabeth, didn't you *hear* me? You're, like, someplace else. Here I am talking about how much I've wanted to be with you and . . . and . . ." Todd bit his lip and hesitated. "And it's like you don't even care," he finished gruffly.

Guilt washed over Elizabeth. The boat took a gentle turn toward an area marked Martian Animal Life—Beware. "I'm sorry," she said. "I understand what you're saying. It's just that—" Her eyes followed the back of Byron's head, which was turning left and right, left and right as he took in all the special effects.

A moment ago Jessica had disappeared from view, but now she was back again. Elizabeth's heart stopped. Byron was going to turn around any minute, she was sure of it. "It's just that," she repeated woodenly, "that . . . What was I saying?"

"Honestly, Elizabeth!" Todd snapped. He folded his arms and stared morosely ahead. "You've been like this practically all day! First the van, then the game room, now here!" He glanced quickly at her, his jaw clenching and unclenching. "Except for that time when I gave you the teddy bear, I've felt like I don't even know you."

"Oh, Todd." Elizabeth felt terrible, but she had to keep her eyes trained on the boat ahead of them. If Byron looked a little to the right at the next turn, he'd see them for sure. Her palms felt sweaty. "I—I don't mean for you to feel bad. I'm just . . ." Her voice trailed off. Darn it, she'd lost her train of thought again.

"Just *what?*" Todd demanded. "If you don't want to hang out with me, Elizabeth, all you have to do is say so and I'll leave. No one's going to accuse Todd Wilkins of hanging around where he isn't wanted!"

"But I *do* want you to hang around," Elizabeth protested. She wished she dared look at him, but she knew she couldn't. What if Byron turned around while her guard was down? If they were caught? She shuddered.

". . . anyway, that's what I think," Todd was saying. "How about *you?*"

Huh? Elizabeth realized she hadn't heard the

beginning of what Todd had said. "I'm—I'm sorry, Todd," she stammered. "I, um, wasn't listening. Could you say that again?"

Todd stood up in one quick motion, and Elizabeth unwillingly tore her eyes away from Byron. There was a sorrowful but angry expression on Todd's face. "Well, I guess that answers my question," he said sadly. "You don't really care about me, do you? You can't be bothered to pay attention to me. I don't have to take this." He glanced to the left, where Elizabeth saw a dimly lit Emergency Exit sign. "I'm out of here. Good-*bye*, Elizabeth Wakefield." In one quick motion he was over the rail of the boat and splashing off into the darkness.

Elizabeth felt like crying. "Darn, darn, darn," she muttered helplessly as the boat moved onward. She'd really done it now. She'd been so worried about *Jessica's* making Todd angry. But she needn't have bothered.

She'd made him mad herself, thank you very much. A big tear rolled down her cheek.

Don't turn around, Jessica thought intently. She aimed her thoughts at Byron, hoping that ESP really worked. *Don't turn around. . . .*

She'd heard all kinds of strange noises from behind her ever since she'd pretended to faint. Some whispered words. Some sounds like people shifting in the seat. Then a splash, then thumping noises, as if somebody was running down the concrete path outside the man-made river, and finally the snuffling sounds of someone crying.

It was like a very quiet soap opera, she told herself grimly.

"Hey, look at that one!" Byron chortled, turning left and right to watch a Martian hawk soar by. "Check out the metallic tail feathers and the fluorescent wings!"

Jessica smiled tightly, but she didn't dare look at it for more than a moment. She knew she'd better keep an eye on Byron instead. "It's, um, nice," she ventured.

"Nice?" Byron frowned. The hawk turned and dived their way. Instinctively Jessica covered her head. "It's totally cool, is what it is. None of this 'nice' garbage. Know how they do that? They have, like, three different state-of-the-art video terminals, and there's a guy who does it all by computer and—Hey, dig the teeth on that woodchuck."

Jessica shuddered. If they had woodchucks like that on Mars, she decided, she'd never leave planet Earth. It looked computerized too, she decided, but she couldn't be sure.

"No, wait a moment," Byron said. "It's not a wood-chuck at all. It's a furry crocodile. With something in its mouth. Ugh, gross." Fascinated, he leaned closer.

"Look over here, Byron," Jessica said, grabbing his shoulder. In another moment the boat would pass the crocodile, and if Byron was still looking at it, he'd—

"Hold on," Byron said. "Hey, check out the way it moves! And listen to that noise!"

Jessica watched in alarm as the boat slid past the

crocodile. Byron's head swiveled steadily backward. The crocodile rose, its jaws suddenly opening, and it let out an unearthly wail, but Jessica scarcely noticed. "Byron!" she shrieked, clutching his arm in pretend terror.

"Hey, take it easy," Byron said. "Whoa, baby! I want one of these on my show, Elizabeth! Talk about cool! Ratings would go through the roof. Look at the way the teeth light up and—"

Jessica thought quickly. She could see only one way out. As the crocodile lunged forward, so did she. With a sudden motion she stood up and leaned to the side. The boat tipped dramatically.

"Help, Byron! The crocodile's got me!" she shrieked, tumbling into the river.

Nine

The Martian Canals tunnel was dark, but Sophia didn't mind a bit. She stood in the back of the loading area. If anyone was chasing her, she'd just dart back even further into the shadows, and they'd never find her.

Unless they had a pair of those infrared goggles that let them see in the dark. And she didn't think the park security guards would. The FBI, maybe, but not the guards.

She chewed at a fingernail. Of course, she wouldn't be able to stay in the ride forever. They'd close the park sooner or later. And she had to go home eventually. But for now, she was happy to be safe.

Still, something weird was definitely going on. A few minutes after she'd hidden, Byron and Elizabeth had come in, gotten into a boat, and started down the stream. Then just a bit later, *Todd* had come in with Elizabeth and done exactly the same thing. Obviously one of them wasn't Elizabeth at all. Obviously one of them was Jessica. Only—Sophia had left Jessica back at school, decorating the gym. Wearing a shirt with a *JW* monogram, not a *Young Love* T-shirt like both of the "Elizabeths" had on.

Well, it was too confusing, and maybe her eyes were just playing tricks on her. Sophia sighed deeply and leaned back against a post—

Just as Patrick and Maria walked in.

Sophia's heart started beating so loudly, she was sure the noise would give her away. Stealing slowly behind the post, she kept her eyes trained directly on them.

"Oh, Maria," Patrick was saying. He held Maria's hand tightly, Sophia noticed with a start. "I am *so* glad I met you."

Sophia's stomach suddenly felt as if it had a rock in it. *He's just acting,* she assured herself nervously. *That's all.*

Still, Patrick did sound awfully sincere. Sophia bit her lip.

Maria said something that Sophia didn't quite catch, but it made Patrick smile. "This ride was a really good choice," he said happily. He helped Maria into the next boat and hopped in too. "We can get to know each other better—in private!"

Sophia's heart did a flip-flop. Marshall was nowhere in sight, so Patrick certainly didn't need to be acting like this—did he? She'd said, "Do whatever it takes," sure, but Patrick didn't have to take her *literally*.

Maria sat back. "We certainly have stuff to talk about," she said.

"Don't I know it!" Patrick sat down by her and trailed a hand in the water. "Off we go—hang on tight!"

The boat slipped slowly away from the loading dock. Sophia crept forward from her hiding place. Her throat felt dry. Had she really heard what she'd thought she'd heard? No, she *couldn't* have. And yet facts were facts. Maria and Patrick were talking as though they were . . . *together*.

Sophia came to a sudden decision. Walking quickly forward, she cut in front of a couple on line. "Excuse me," she said, "but I've been standing here forever." Then she climbed into the next boat. Gentle waves lapped at the side of the boat. Sophia crouched as low as she could and kept her eyes fixed on the couple ahead of her.

Marshall might be the *Young Love* spy, but it was time she did a little spying of her own.

"That was, um, a fun ride," Jessica said, not quite looking at Byron. She wrung a little water out of her shirt as he helped her onto the exit dock.

"I hope you didn't get too wet," Byron said. "At least it was just water and not soda, like this morning." He grinned. "I guess this is what you call an interactive ride, huh? Where the Martians try to eat you? Good thing I was there to fish you out of the water—even though it was only six inches deep."

And good thing it kept you from noticing who was behind us, Jessica thought. Still, they weren't safe yet. The boat behind them was about to dock, and the boat behind *that* had Elizabeth in it.

"Interested in a video of your trip?" an attendant asked, flashing them a bright smile. She pointed to a display. "You're number seven-fifty-three. You can buy a complete video for seven-ninety-five plus tax, or a regular photograph for just five dollars plus tax."

"Well, now . . ." Byron's hand snaked to his pocket, and he looked questioningly at Jessica.

Jessica swallowed hard. Not only did she look like a dweeb in the picture labeled 753, but the photo labeled 755 showed Elizabeth—the real Elizabeth. She thought fast. "I don't think so," she said, pulling Byron by the hand. "Let's try out the Ferris wheel instead. Maybe it'll dry me out a little."

"Sounds great!" Byron's face broke into a sunny smile.

Breathing a sigh of relief, Jessica led Byron out into the light.

Maria cleared her throat. The boat was winding its way past a luminous skeleton that didn't fool her for a minute. It felt like the right time to have that conversation. "Listen, Patrick," she began.

"Anything for my sweet!" Patrick patted her hand and glanced left and right, as if looking for somebody. "Hey, how long is this ride, anyhow?"

Maria pulled her hand away. What difference did

it make how long the ride was? It was time to be completely open. "You're a wonderful guy and everything," she said, "and I'm so pleased you picked me as your date. It made me feel like I fit in. But I've got to say this, Patrick. I don't think of you in a—"

Patrick whirled to stare directly at her. Maria broke off. He looked downright panic-stricken. "Don't say that!" he whispered, staring quickly down the tunnel.

Maria hadn't expected that reaction. "Oh, Patrick," she said softly. "I *like* you, I really do. But not romantica—"

"Shhh!" Patrick clapped his hand over Maria's mouth. "You don't understand!" he hissed. "You can't *say* that!" He raised his voice. "I'm so glad you feel the same way about me as I feel about you!" he called out, the sound echoing throughout the tunnel.

What in the world? Maria was angry now. Patrick had no right to grab her and say things that weren't even true. She shoved his hand off her mouth and glared at him. But before she could speak, she heard a sudden sob from directly behind them.

"Sophia!" Patrick said in astonishment, turning in his seat. "What are you—I mean—" His body stiffened. "Um, hi," he said weakly.

"I can't believe you're doing this!" Sophia stood up in her boat, eyes blazing.

Maria's head whirled. *Huh?* She narrowed her eyes, trying to figure out what was going on. "Sophia—" she began.

"I—I—" Patrick held out a hand toward Sophia,

but looked nervously to the front of the ride at the same time.

Sophia's eyes filled with tears. Jumping out of the boat, she landed in the middle of a whirlpool marked Dangerous Frogs. "I never want to talk to you again as long as I live. I never want to *see* you again!" Breaking into sobs once more, Sophia darted onto the sidewalk and toward the exit sign.

"Oh, man," Patrick said uncomfortably. "I didn't mean . . ." His voice trailed off. "Um—it's like this, Maria. . . ."

Suddenly everything was clear. "You knew she was back there, didn't you?" Maria snapped. "You *jerk!* You were just trying to make her jealous! Well, I happen to *like* Sophia, and I'm not going to let you hurt her." She stood up and faced Patrick, her hands on her hips. "If you think I'm going to let you use me to make her jealous, you've got another thing coming!"

"Sit down!" Patrick stared in front of him. "It's not what you think. Anyway, we're almost at the exit."

"What does that have to do with the anything?" Maria demanded. She was so angry, she could hardly see. To be nice, she'd gone and hung out with Patrick, when all she wanted was to be with Marshall. To be *nice!* And instead she'd helped hurt one of her best friends in Sweet Valley. "And what do you mean, it's not what I think? What else could it possibly be?" If Marshall hadn't been waiting for her at the end of the ride, she'd have jumped off her own boat.

"It's not true," Patrick said miserably. Ahead of

them the tunnel grew lighter. Patrick's body stiffened. "Look—there's Marshall! Hold my hand! Quick!"

Maria snatched it away. She could catch a quick glimpse of Marshall now, standing on the dock about twenty yards ahead of them. "Do you think I'm *nuts* or something?"

"Listen!" Patrick's voice was frantic but firm. "Marshall isn't who he says he is, OK? He's not Byron's cousin. He's a spy."

"A *what?*" Maria glared at Patrick. "You're going to have to do better than *that*."

"I'm *serious!*" Patrick twisted his hands together. "He's a spy, and he's trying to take away the school dance tonight! See, we cheated and—"

Maria frowned. "You what?"

Patrick glanced at the approaching dock. "We cheated," he repeated, his voice low. "Sophia and me. Well, we tried to, anyway. Remember, I got to pick from you and Sophia and somebody else?"

Maria nodded. "Yeah. So?"

"Sophia and I, we made up a password thing," Patrick explained, looking embarrassed. "Only I forgot it and I didn't pick Sophia." He stared at the bottom of the boat. "I picked you instead. And no offense or anything, Maria, but it was all an accident. But we can't let the *Young Love* people know that we tried to rig the game, or they'll take away our prizes and—"

"Take away our prizes?" Maria yelled. "Is that all you care about?" Her mind raced. So Patrick hadn't picked her because he liked her, or even because he liked her answers. He'd picked her because he thought he was picking Sophia. "You picked me by *mistake?*"

Patrick cast a nervous glance toward Marshall. "Keep it down, OK?"

Maria wasn't about to keep it down. Why should she? She'd never been so hurt in her entire life. Being chosen was all a mistake. And Patrick had been only pretending to like her ever since then.

And as for Marshall—well, he was just pretending to like her too. To get evidence against Patrick.

The boat docked suddenly. They were at the end of the ride. Humiliated, Maria jumped out of the boat and ran toward the exit. "Who *cares* about your old dance, anyway?" she yelled furiously at Patrick as she stomped off.

"Like to buy a video of your trip?" the attendant asked. "Only seven ninety-five plus—"

"Hey, Maria!" Marshall called anxiously. "Are you all right?"

Maria slogged on. One guy who pretended to like her was just cheating on a game show. The other was a spy. She wished she'd never come to Sweet Valley. She wished she'd never *heard* of *Young Love.*

"Leave me alone, you creeps!" she called back over her shoulder, bursting into tears just as she ran out of the Martian Canals and into the bright light of the sunny day.

Ten

Almost blinded by tears, Elizabeth ran for the park entrance. She felt terrible, awful, miserable. Poor Todd. And it was all her fault, no question about it. If only she'd paid attention to Todd when he'd been talking.

If only she hadn't trusted Jessica.

If only she hadn't chickened out when she'd been chosen to be a *Young Love* contestant.

But there was no way to make it better now. *I might as well go home before I make everything worse,* she thought sadly.

She dashed through the line waiting for the merry-go-round, in her haste nearly bowling over a woman and her two little boys. "Sorry!" she called out. She hoped there'd be a bus soon. Right now she was just as happy that she and Jessica had agreed to switch back for the ride home.

All she wanted to do was go home, get into bed, pull the covers up around her, and never come out again.

I can't believe him! Sophia thought as she hurried for the park entrance and the bus stop. Patrick was a jerk, that was all there was to it. Or—wait a minute—there was another word. A word she'd heard in English class once, to describe a guy who tried to have two girlfriends at once. Some retro kind of word. It began with a *C*. . . .

Cad. That was it. Patrick was a cad.

She wiped tears off her cheeks and hurried on. She'd given *weeks* of her life to Patrick, and this was how he repaid her. By cozying up to Maria. And she didn't believe him, not for a minute, when he said he was just doing what she'd told him to do. Even though she'd told him to say what great chemistry he and Maria had, she hadn't told him to *mean* it.

Turning a corner, Sophia came face-to-face with a crowd of children who looked vaguely familiar.

"Thophia!" A runny-nosed little girl glared at her accusingly. "I couldn't find you *anywhere!*"

"Hi," Sophia said weakly, feeling her heart drop to her feet. But there was nothing to do except keep going. "Bye!" she added, sprinting through a sudden break in the crowd.

She hoped a bus would be waiting.

All she wanted to do was cry herself to sleep in her own bed.

*   *   *

Maria slid onto a bench in front of the game room. She could still feel her teeth clenching and unclenching. She'd never been so humiliated in her entire life. Taking deep breaths, she wondered what to do next.

Taking the van back to school was out of the question. No way would she sit next to Patrick, or even in the same *vehicle* as Patrick. Not after what he'd done to her. And if that meant everyone would miss the dance, so what? A fat lot *Maria* cared. It wasn't really her school anyway. She was a newcomer and she was unwelcome—anybody could see that. It wasn't as if any of the kids *liked* her or anything.

She stared morosely at the entrance to the game room. Fun! Great Games! Great Prizes! the sign by the entrance read. Maria sighed. Fun was exactly what she *wasn't* having right now.

And the worst of it was, she'd had such high hopes. Earlier today, it had looked as though she'd won two great prizes: Marshall and Patrick. But both of them had turned out to be total twerps.

Amy and Aaron strolled slowly out the game room door, loaded down with stuffed animals and prizes of all kinds. Maria raised her eyebrows. Not only were they talking, they were laughing and joking too. This wasn't making any sense.

"Hi, Maria!" Amy and Aaron came over to the bench. "Having fun?"

"No," Maria said shortly.

Amy frowned. "Where's Patrick?"

Maria shrugged. It was easier than saying, "I don't know and I *certainly* don't care."

"Something's wrong." Amy put some of her stuffed animals down and sat on the bench. "Do you want to talk about it?"

Maria shook her head violently. No, she did *not* want to talk about it. Not even a little bit. Not even with Amy, who was probably the closest thing to a friend she had in Sweet Valley.

"Well, OK," Amy said, patting Maria on the shoulder. "Do you want a teddy bear or something?"

"No," Maria said, and then, to be polite, she added, "Thank you."

"I won a bunch of stuff," Amy explained. "So did Aaron. In fact, we won so many animals, we kind of lost track." She laughed. "We were having a contest, and I guess we both won."

"I didn't know you were so coordinated," Aaron said, grinning. "We should get together sometime and play basketball."

"You're on!" Amy said happily. "You know what's really weird?" she asked Maria. "Donald and Janet. Even *they've* been having a great time. Donald's really good at popping balloons with laser beams, and Janet was really impressed, and they've been working together to beat this game with plastic disks and—"

This was absolutely too much. "Donald and *Janet* are getting along?" Maria asked, her eyes brimming with tears. Donald and Janet could become friends, but nobody wanted to be with

Maria. Except if they were spies. Or if they made a mistake.

"Yeah," Aaron said. "They've been inseparable."

Maria sighed. *Inseparable.* Everybody but her. "Have you seen Todd and Elizabeth?" she asked glumly.

Amy made a face. "That's the other strange thing. Something happened, I don't know what, and Todd's just sitting in the middle of the game room looking upset. As for Elizabeth, I don't know. Todd won't talk about it."

Maria couldn't believe what she was hearing. The situation didn't make any sense. The two couples who'd been excited about being together weren't speaking. The two couples who'd hated each other this morning and almost refused to go on the trip were having a great time.

"Well, we'll see you back at the van, Maria," Aaron said importantly, pulling Amy off to the other side of the bench. "Me and Ame are going to hit the roller coaster."

"See you later, Maria," Amy said. "Hope you feel better soon." She turned to Aaron. "Race you!" she giggled, and they were off.

"Hope you feel better soon," Maria repeated under her breath. *No, you don't,* she thought sadly. *Not really.* Even Amy was more interested in Aaron than in her, she decided. She choked back a sob. Even Amy didn't truly care about Maria. Just like everybody else at Sweet Valley Middle

School, when you came right down to it.

A tear trickled down Maria's cheek.

She felt completely unloved. Unloved and unappreciated. How could she have fooled herself? She'd never fit in.

Never.

Getting slowly to her feet, she turned and headed for the entrance and the city bus.

"So what is it with you Sweet Valley kids, anyway?" Marshall demanded. He stood in the door of the *Young Love* van and glared at Jessica.

Jessica sat up in surprise. "What do you mean?" she asked. She was seated with Byron in the front row of the van, busily ignoring Todd, who was sulking in the seat behind them. It was almost time for the van to leave, and most of the *Young Love* couples were already there—in addition to all the stuffed animals Amy and Aaron had won, which filled an entire seat in the back row.

"You know what I mean." Marshall shook his head tiredly. "Remember? You got off that Martian Canals ride and you looked kind of upset. And I thought I'd be a nice guy and say, 'Hi, didn't I see you on the van?' and you didn't even glance my way. You completely dissed me."

Jessica wondered what to say. Marshall must have run into Elizabeth, she realized, but she couldn't say that, or else Byron would know something was up. "Um—" she began.

"And then there was that other one, the girl I saw with Patrick and Maria earlier today," Marshall went on. "I don't know her name." ·

"Sophia," Patrick said gloomily. Jessica turned around and saw that he was sitting alone too. Where was Maria? she wondered.

"Yeah, Sophia," Marshall agreed. "I saw her too. Later on. She was sitting on a bench, crying a little, and I thought I'd be a nice guy, say, 'How are you, and is anything wrong?' and she just jumped down my throat! She screamed, 'As if I would tell *you* anything!' She acted like I had a *disease*. She was just as nasty as you were, Elizabeth. Worse. You guys are all alike." He dropped into the nearest seat. "If it were up to me, Byron, I'd cancel the dance."

Sophia? Jessica mused. But what would Sophia have been doing here? "Well, how about Maria?" she asked, hoping to cheer Marshall up. "Last I saw, you guys were getting along real well."

Marshall snorted. "I *thought* we were. Then she went ballistic on me for no reason. One minute it's 'Oh, Marshall, it's so cool how we both like the same old movies!' And the next it's 'Hey, Marshall, you're a jerk! I can't stand you!'" He ran his hand through his hair. "Well, if you guys are all like that, it's a good thing I don't go to school here."

"Five minutes," Ms. Sylvester announced. "Everybody on board? Where's Donald Zweebling and his sweetiecakes?"

Jessica grinned. She stared out the window. "Here they are," she reported as Donald and Janet drew near, their arms loaded with stuffed animals and other prizes. To Jessica's surprise, they were talking excitedly together. She strained to make out their voices.

". . . so I'll come over to your house next Thursday and show you what I mean," Donald was saying.

"That'd be great," Janet replied.

Jessica raised her eyebrows in surprise. Donald Zwerdling and Janet Howell. Not that they were behaving like a couple or anything, but still, to have them even recognize that the other one existed—well, that was pretty amazing.

"So is that everybody?" Ms. Sylvester demanded.

Byron turned around in his seat. "Buddy check. Amy and Aaron!"

"Here!" Amy and Aaron sang out.

"Elizabeth and Todd!"

"Here!" Jessica cried, her arm shooting into the air.

"Here," Todd muttered.

"Patrick and Maria!"

There was silence.

"Patrick and Maria?" Byron half rose from his seat.

"Well, I'm here," Patrick said with a sigh. "But I don't know where Maria is. I haven't seen her in a long time."

Marshall grunted. "Who cares anyway?"

Jessica licked her lips. She cared anyway. She cared a lot. Because if Maria didn't come back with Patrick, then there wouldn't be any dance.

Ms. Sylvester glanced at her watch. "She'd better turn up within five minutes," she said gleefully. "Because—"

She started up the engine with a roar and looked into the rearview mirror with a satisfied grin. "If she doesn't make it, your school dance is *history!*"

Elizabeth sat on the bus, willing it to go. According to the schedule, it was supposed to sit at the Dizzy Planet stop for exactly five minutes before leaving, and she was certain that at least five minutes had already passed. Maybe ten. In fact, it might even have been a few hours.

She promised herself that she would never, ever come back to this theme park again. Too many bad memories. Gluing her eyes to the door of the bus so she wouldn't have to look out the window, she watched an elderly woman climb on board, then a young family, then a teenage boy in a tattered shirt and baggy shorts, and then—

Wait a minute.

Elizabeth blinked. A girl was darting into the aisle, breathing heavily as if she'd been running. Sophia Rizzo. But what was Sophia doing here?

Sophia stopped short. "Elizabeth!" she said, astonished. "I mean, Jessica!" She frowned. "Who are you?" she asked guardedly.

Elizabeth knew the time for pretending was past. Anyway, she realized, if she told Sophia the truth, she might feel a little better. Sometimes talking about problems did that, she'd noticed. "I'm Elizabeth," she said heavily. "Hi, Sophia."

Sophia blinked and pushed a few strands of hair out of her eyes. Behind her, the door slid shut with a hiss. "But—what are you doing here?" she asked.

Elizabeth slid over and patted the seat beside her. "Sit down," she told her friend. "It's a long story."

Fortunately, the ride home would be long enough to tell the whole thing.

"T minus six seconds and counting," Ms. Sylvester said pleasantly. "T minus three seconds . . ."

Jessica held her breath and stared out the window, willing Maria to appear.

"T minus zero seconds," Ms. Sylvester announced. "Too bad. You lose." She put the van into gear with a thunk. Jessica felt her stomach lurch forward.

"Oh, but we can't!" Amy burst out.

"Fair's fair," Ms. Sylvester drawled. "You knew the rules, and so did she. If she doesn't follow them, it's not my problem." She signaled to pull into traffic. "You don't like it, blame her. Tear her apart Monday morning when she gets to school. Or poison her milk. Either way."

Jessica sat transfixed. "But—but—" she stammered.

Donald stood up. "Please, Ms. Sylvester," he said politely. "Would you just wait for ten more minutes? Maria may have lost track of the time, you know." He smiled at her. "It does happen."

Ms. Sylvester snorted. "Ten minutes, huh?" She

stared hard at Donald in the rearview mirror. "All right. Ten minutes. But no more. And only because you asked so nicely, Donald Zwiplash." She paused. "And because I like your last name."

Donald grinned.

Ten minutes. Jessica swallowed hard, trying not to think of the dance. What if it was canceled? Well, the way things were going, that might not be such a bad thing. Of course, Jessica wasn't counting on the rest of the school feeling that way.

She shook her head glumly. Ten minutes.

Jessica stuck her nose back against the window glass.

"Maria had just *better* show up," she muttered under her breath.

"So we both cheated, I guess," Sophia said, trying to smile at Elizabeth. It was strange how good it felt to get the truth out into the open. Now that she'd told Elizabeth what she'd done, she didn't feel quite so worried about getting caught.

"I guess," Elizabeth echoed. "I feel bad about that, Sophia, but mostly I feel bad about Todd. I know he'll never want to speak to me again." She turned to stare out the window. "And it's all my fault."

Sophia touched her friend's arm. "Maybe you can make it up to him somehow," she said. "Everybody has a bad day now and then. And you've actually got a built-in excuse. Just tell him you're really sorry about what happened at the theme park. And then tell him you just weren't yourself that day." Sophia grinned. "And in fact, you *weren't* yourself—so it's even true."

"Todd, I'm so sorry about yesterday," Elizabeth said slowly. "I know I really hurt your feelings, but I just wasn't myself." She looked up at Sophia, her lips curving into a smile. "You know, it might just work."

"I'm *sure* it'll work," Sophia said. "Todd is such a nice guy, I know he won't hold it against you." She sighed. "If only I could figure out what to do about Patrick! When I saw him with Maria that way, it was like a knife stabbing into my heart."

Elizabeth frowned. "Wait a minute. You told Patrick to show Marshall that he and Maria were together, right?"

Sophia nodded. "But when I saw them in the tunnel, Marshall wasn't anywhere around." Her stomach knotted itself together again. "The other stuff I could take, but when Marshall wasn't even *there*—"

Elizabeth held up a finger. "Oh, but he *was*," she said.

"He was?" Sophia looked doubtfully at her friend. "How do you know?"

"Because he was standing there on the exit dock when I got out of the boat," Elizabeth said. "He's the guy you were talking to this morning with Patrick and Maria, right? Tall, blond, clothes that don't fit?"

"Yeah," Sophia agreed, "but—"

Elizabeth spread out her hands. "Then it's simple," she said. "Patrick must have told Marshall to wait for them at the other end, so he and Maria could go for a ride together and seem like they were really a couple. But Patrick didn't know where the ride ended, and so he wasn't taking any chances." She raised an eyebrow. "He kept talking about how much he liked Maria the whole ride through, just in case Marshall could hear them. "

Sophia colored. She thought back to the Martian Canals. Now that she considered it, Patrick *had* been talking loudly. As if he wanted to be overheard. And he'd kept looking toward the front of the ride, as if waiting to see Marshall. . . .

"And they film all the rides at Dizzy Planet," Elizabeth went on. "Every time I went through a ride, they'd try to sell me the video. And you can see the videos from the ride exit, so Patrick probably thought Marshall was watching him and Maria on the video display screen."

Sophia's heart gave a tiny leap. "Maybe you're right," she said in a small voice.

"Of course I'm right," Elizabeth said. "So it sounds like we both have to apologize."

Sophia nodded. *Apologize.* It would be hard, but she knew she could do it. If Elizabeth was right.

She felt a small flicker of hope.

"And you're lucky too," Elizabeth said, "because Patrick is such a nice guy, he won't hold it against you. In fact, he might even be flattered." She chuckled. "Just say, 'Patrick, I got so jealous when I saw you with Maria.'"

"I got so jealous when I saw you with Maria,"

Sophia repeated, taking a deep breath. *It just might work.* "Because we're the ones who've got—" She hesitated, searching for the right word.

"Chemistry?" Elizabeth supplied.

Of course! "Yeah, chemistry," Sophia said with relief.

Eleven

So the dance will be canceled, Maria thought. She stood huddled by the bus stop just outside the Dizzy Planet entrance gate, waiting for a city bus. *Good. They don't like me here, and that's OK, because I don't like them either.*

It was just a shame about Marshall. He had such a great personality. Or so she'd *thought*.

A shadow fell across her face. She looked up in surprise to see Amy Sutton standing over her.

"There you are," Amy said. "I kind of thought I'd find you here. Come on. The van's waiting for you."

"I'm not going." Maria shook her head. "And you can't make me."

"I know you're upset," Amy said gently. "Sometime maybe you'll tell me why. It has something to do with Marshall, I know that. If it's any consolation, he's kind of upset too."

"If he told you that, he's a pretty good actor," Maria muttered, wishing Amy would leave her in peace. "And so is *Patrick*." She spat out Patrick's name as if he had rabies.

"Actors," Amy mused aloud. "Let's talk about actors. You know, when you first moved to Sweet Valley, some people said you were a stuck-up jerk. Not because they knew you, but because you were a child actor." She looked meaningfully at Maria. "Because everybody *knows* that actors are selfish and bratty."

"So what's your point?" Maria grumbled.

"Well, I was scared to get to know you at first," Amy went on. "I mean, who wants to be friends with a brat? But I tried, and I discovered something interesting." She leaned closer to Maria. "You aren't like that at all."

"Hold on." Maria held up a hand. "I'm not just *saying* that Marshall and Patrick are jerks. I have *proof*."

"Fine," Amy said with a shrug. "I'm not talking about Marshall and Patrick. I'm talking about *you*. Maria Slater. And the people who said you'd never fit in at Sweet Valley Middle School, the people who said that all actors are spoiled and snobby and show-offs. And I didn't think it was true."

Maria felt a sudden stab of guilt. She took a deep breath. No. She wouldn't listen to what Amy had to say. She wouldn't. She would *not*—

"So, here's what I want to know," Amy said quietly. In the distance Maria could see the bus approaching. "The van leaves for school in, let me see, three minutes. You can be on it and prove that I was right.

Or you can take the bus and be the reason they cancel the dance, and—well, I guess you can figure out the rest." She folded her arms and smiled at Maria. "But it's your choice. Which will it be?"

Oh, no. Maria made a tight line with her lips. She wished Amy hadn't brought up the whole Hollywood business. What had she said about Patrick earlier that day? Her voice echoed in her head: *"He wasn't worried that I was a selfish spoiled brat."* Maria's shoulders sagged.

And all at once she knew she didn't have a choice.

She *was* being selfish. Selfish and bratty and mean. No matter what Marshall and Patrick had done to her, she owed it to all the other kids not to be the reason their dance was canceled.

Embarrassed, Maria looked at the ground. If she wanted to be part of the group, to make real friends, then she had to show people like Amy that they were right to believe in her.

Which meant that she had to get to the van. And get there *now.*

"Let's go!" she said, grasping Amy's hand.

"All right!" Amy pumped her fist in the air. "I knew you'd come through, Maria! Anyway, if you didn't, I'd have poisoned your milk Monday morning."

Maria didn't bother to laugh. She headed as quickly as she could across the parking lot.

She only hoped they'd make it in time.

*   *   *

"One minute," Ms. Sylvester announced. She fixed Donald with a look. "And no more extensions, Mr. Zwieback."

Jessica bit her nails and looked frantically out the window. Amy had sounded awfully sure of herself a few minutes earlier when she'd left the van to go find Maria. "I can get her," she'd said, and Jessica had believed her.

Now it looked like they'd be heading back to school minus *two* people.

"Byron, can't you do something?" she pleaded. "You're the host. It's not fair, really it isn't."

Byron smiled. "That's young love," he said in his best host's voice. "Sometimes it works out, and sometimes it doesn't."

"Oh, you're no help." Jessica turned away sadly.

"Forty-five seconds!" Ms. Sylvester sang out.

Byron patted down his hair. "Well, actually, there *is* something we could try," he said, smiling brightly at Jessica. "Repeat after me, OK?" He held his right hand up in the air.

"OK," Jessica agreed, holding up her own hand, though for the life of her she couldn't figure out what this would do.

"Under penalty of public humiliation," Byron droned.

"Under penalty of public humiliation," Jessica repeated as quickly as she could.

"I, state your name," Byron continued.

"I, state your—" Jessica broke off. *No, you idiot*, she told herself sternly. *He means I should say my name.* "I, Jessica Wakefield," she corrected.

There was a sudden silence.

"Go on," Jessica urged, leaning forward. "What else, Byron?"

Byron grinned widely. "Tell me, *Elizabeth*—what did you just say your name was?"

Jessica froze. Then she sagged against the back of the seat, her heart pounding. How could she have fallen for that? How could she have been so *stupid?* "I meant to say Elizabeth!" she said quickly. "Of course I'm Elizabeth. I've been Elizabeth for, like, my whole life!" She forced a laugh. Maybe she could convince Byron that her slip of the tongue was a big joke. "No—wait—I'm kidding!"

Byron gestured to her. "Meet Jessica Wakefield, folks! I knew it all along."

Todd stood up sharply. "Jessica? What the—" His mouth hung open.

"Twenty seconds," Ms. Sylvester droned.

"You can't cancel the dance," Jessica argued, fear rising in her throat. "You can't! We didn't exactly *cheat,* we just—I mean . . ." She thought frantically.

"You mean it was you the whole—" Todd began.

"Who said anything about canceling the dance?" Byron said, still grinning. "Whoever you are, you came with Todd this morning and you're going back with him now. That's in the rules. We wouldn't cancel the dance over *that.* We'd only cancel the dance if Amy and Maria don't show—"

There was a scuffling sound outside the van, and

the door flew wide open. Amy stepped in, holding Maria by the hand. "Are we on time?" she asked.

"T minus ten seconds and counting," Ms. Sylvester chanted.

"And they did," Byron finished, nodding toward Maria. "Glad you made it. Everybody ready for the dance of the decade?"

"Ladies and gentlemen!" Byron called into the mike. He was standing onstage in the gym later that evening, dressed in a tux with a *Young Love* button on his lapel. "We have a special surprise for you, so if you'll just quit dancing for thirty seconds or so . . ."

The music died and the couples on the dance floor parted. There were some good-natured boos. Elizabeth stood in the back near Sophia, grasping the teddy bear Todd had given her. She'd changed out of her T-shirt and was watching the stage anxiously for a glimpse of Todd. The couples still hadn't come out.

"Thanks a lot," Byron said. "First I'd like to introduce tonight's winning couples! Maestro?" He motioned to the band, which burst into a series of loud chords. "Amy Sutton and Aaron Dallas!"

The audience cheered. Aaron sauntered onto the stage, holding up Amy's hand as if she'd won a boxing match. "Thank you, thank you!" he called out, bowing low.

"If I were Amy, I'd kick him in the behind," Sophia whispered.

Elizabeth smiled. Instead, Amy had started bowing

too. They bowed their way across to the far corner of the stage.

"Next," Byron said, "Donald Zwerdling and Janet Howell!"

There were more loud chords. Donald ambled out, looking embarrassed. Janet guided him to their spot, waving grandly to the other students.

Sophia nudged Elizabeth. "Just like a queen," she murmured.

"What else do you expect from Janet?" Elizabeth murmured back.

"Our third couple," Byron said, his voice crackling over the mike, "is a mystery couple. It's—" He paused. "Todd Wilkins and either Elizabeth or Jessica Wakefield!"

Elizabeth blinked. So Byron knew. She watched her sister, blushing furiously, walk across the stage a few paces behind Todd, who was looking steadfastly toward the ground. Her heart soared. If Byron knew, then Todd knew—and maybe that meant everything would be easier to explain.

Elizabeth shook her head as Byron wrapped up his introductions. Love was tough to figure out, that was for sure.

"So what's the surprise?" Winston Egbert called out.

Byron grinned and motioned behind him. On cue, an enormous movie screen rolled down from the ceiling. The lights dimmed. "I've been working on a new show for the network," he said into the mike, his voice smooth as silk. "And you're getting a sneak preview."

A sneak preview? Curious, Elizabeth leaned forward.

"Love is such an interesting thing," Byron said, winking at the contestants onstage. "When a date is good, it's very, very good. When it's bad, it's bogus! I've always wanted to know what goes on behind the scenes of a really smelly date." He paused. "So I hid a few cameras around the theme park today. And placed one or two on my van. And dropped a few hints here and there." He smiled, showing all his teeth. "Ladies and gentlemen, welcome to the pilot episode of *Dating: It's the Pits!*"

Elizabeth licked her lips nervously. If there were hidden cameras in the park, they might have gotten pictures of her switching places with her sister. They might have gotten the Martian Canals ride. . . . She gulped.

Light flickered on the screen. Elizabeth stared. The picture was of the van, parked outside the school earlier that morning. There was Donald staring worshipfully up at Janet while Janet looked in the other direction as hard as she could.

"That's not funny!" Janet cried from the stage.

Elizabeth couldn't help a laugh. Neither could Sophia, next to her.

Theme music poured through the loudspeakers. "Well, it's comin' up on a Saturday night," Byron sang in a country twang, "and you don't want to be alone. You look around for a date that's right, and you pick up the telephone."

The scene shifted. Elizabeth swallowed hard. There was Todd, trying desperately to hook his arm around Jessica in the van, while Jessica twisted and turned every which way to avoid it. Laughter filled the audience.

"Smooth moves, Toddster!" Winston shouted out.

"And you find a guy that you barely know," Byron went on, "and you hope he's not a ditz."

Elizabeth shook her head sadly. Poor Todd. Poor, poor Todd. She resolved that she would never again switch identities with her sister if it meant fooling Todd.

"'Cause the date could be great if you know where to go," Byron added, his voice reaching a crescendo, "or the date could be the pits!"

The audience roared. The scene shifted again. This time Elizabeth saw herself decorating the gym with Sophia while the two *Young Love* workers walked by, talking about someone having cheated.

"Oh, my gosh . . ." Sophia bit her lip. On the screen both girls had nearly jumped out of their skins. Now they were babbling so fast they could hardly understand the words. "We were pretty obvious, huh?"

Elizabeth took a deep breath. "I'll say," she murmured. *When they said they were going to catch the cheaters,* she thought suddenly, *they just meant that they were going to catch them on video—not with spies!* She stared in fascination as the scenes went on, one after the other: Maria walking between Patrick and Marshall, her head swiveling back and forth as she tried to speak to both of them at once; Jessica throwing herself into the Martian canal and Byron fishing her out from the grasp of the high-tech furry crocodile; Janet and Donald in the game room, starting far apart and gradually getting closer and closer as their competition progressed; Sophia sneaking into the park, holding a runny-nosed little girl's hand, and then Sophia a little later, peering out from behind a trash can near the Monster Splash.

Elizabeth flinched every time she appeared on the screen, but after a few minutes she began to enjoy it. It was funny, after all—even the parts involving her. And she especially liked the way Byron had tricked her sister into saying her real name. When the video came to an end, everybody clapped. Byron bowed.

"Thank you, thank you!" he said, holding up both his arms in triumph. "Looks like we may have a winner here." Then he dropped his voice. "But there's a serious lesson to be learned tonight, besides all the fun. And that's a message about love."

The gym went silent. Byron paced back and forth, looking over the couples on the stage in front of him.

"We all try to rig the game of love," he said smoothly, as though thinking aloud. "Everybody does it—you, me, all of us. A few people up here on the stage tried to, um, rig things a little more than most." Even from a distance, Elizabeth could see Jessica and Patrick blush. The audience began to laugh.

"But," Byron said, holding up a finger, "it can't be done. And I think we've seen that here tonight. Love's like a river, folks. We can build dams to try to control it, but the river always does what it wants in the end. And love is the same way." He grinned broadly. "Will

*   *   *

"We're sorry, Maria," Sophia said humbly. "We should never have put you through—well, you know."

Maria did know, all right. She stared at Sophia and Patrick without moving. Everybody else looked as though they were having a blast ever since the dancing had begun a while earlier, but she was still miserable, and angry at everybody. At Sophia. At Patrick. And at Marshall.

Especially at Marshall.

"Oh, it's all right," she muttered. She looked bleakly across the sea of dancers enjoying themselves. The weird thing was, she couldn't get Marshall out of her brain. Every time she thought she ought to just grab a partner and go out to the floor, something stopped her. And she was pretty sure that the something was a guy with blond hair, slightly ripped jeans, and a fondness for old romantic comedies.

Byron danced over with Jessica. "Have some fun!" he cried out. "Go find Marshall, Maria! Ask him to dance. Where's he hiding, anyhow?"

"How should I know where he is?" Maria demanded. "Where do spies hang out anyway?"

Byron stopped dancing so quickly Jessica almost lost her balance. "Spies? What are you talking about?"

"You know perfectly well," Maria snapped. "Spies. Like Marshall." She looked to Sophia and Patrick for help. "He was trying to find out who was cheating and—"

She broke off. Byron was shaking his head in

disbelief. "A *spy?* Marshall? No, no—I was the only spy at Dizzy Planet. Me and the hidden cameras."

"But of course he was a spy," Patrick argued. "Sophia told me so." He turned to stare at Sophia.

Maria had an uncomfortable feeling in her stomach. "Well, if he isn't a spy, what *is* he?"

"Didn't he tell you?" Byron groaned. "He's my—"

"Your *cousin,*" Sophia said sourly. "That's what he told us, anyway. But we knew better. He said it with a stumble, like this." She imitated Marshall's voice. " 'I'm Byron's, um, cousin.' Like that."

"Yeah," Patrick agreed. "With the 'um.' That was suspicious, all right."

"He *isn't* my cousin," Byron said casually. "But he isn't a spy either. He's my nephew. Oh, I know he's only a couple of years younger than me. My oldest sister was twenty when I was born, so . . ." He shrugged. "Anyway, Marshall likes to say he's my cousin, because no one ever believes him when he says he's my nephew." He laughed. "Uncle Byron. Can you *imagine?*"

Maria breathed deeply. "So what was he doing on the van, then?"

"Just what he told you—going along for the ride." Byron winked at Jessica. "Boy, talk about suspicious!" he said, then whirled back into the crowd. "So long, guys! See you in the funny papers!"

"Oops," Sophia said after a moment. She laid her hand on Maria's. "I guess I blew it, huh?"

"I guess we all did," Maria murmured. Her stomach was in turmoil. She stole a quick look to her right.

Through the doorway she could see the *Young Love* van in the parking lot.

Sophia cleared her throat. "Um—Maria—"

"Listen, I'll catch you guys later," Maria said quickly. She darted away from Sophia and Patrick and headed for the door.

Maybe she'd be in luck.

"Well, if it isn't Maria See-ya-later!" Ms. Sylvester said. She leaned out the window of the driver's seat and narrowed her eyes. "The one who nearly got the dance canceled all by her lonesome. Cute move, kid. So what do you want?"

Maria swallowed hard. "Um—Ms. Sylvester," she said hesitantly, "um—I wondered . . . do you know where Marshall went?"

"Marshall?" Ms. Sylvester's eyebrows shot straight up. "You mean Marshall the famous nephew? Marshall, who's been sitting around muttering about how Sweet Valley kids are all losers? You mean *that* Marshall?"

"Um . . . yeah," Maria agreed. "I learned something interesting a minute ago. And it kind of, um, changed things."

Ms. Sylvester laughed sourly. "Get in," she said, pressing a switch. The door slid open. "I asked him if he wanted to hit the dance, but he just growled at me. At *me*. Can you imagine?"

Maria couldn't, in fact. "Thanks, Ms. Sylvester," she said gratefully, and climbed aboard. "Marshall?" she asked. "Are you here?"

For a moment there was silence. Then a cold voice sounded from the back of the van. "Go away."

Maria stood on tiptoe. Marshall was sprawled across the backseat, the one where he and Maria had sat on the way to Dizzy Planet. A paperback book was open in front of him. "It's me, Maria," she said gently. "Listen, Marshall. I've come to, um, apologize. And to ask if you wanted to come into the gym and dance with me."

"Yeah, right." Marshall rolled over and looked up, his expression sullen. "Tell me another one."

"I'm serious." Maria tried to catch Marshall's eye. "I treated you badly, and I'd . . . well, I'd like to dance with you," she repeated.

Marshall gave a little shrug. "That dance isn't for *me*," he said. "It's for the snobs like you who go *here*. To Sweet Valley Middle School. The losingest bunch of stuck-up dorks I've ever met in my entire life. Patrick, Elizabeth, Sophia . . ." He ticked people off on his fingers. "I don't belong there."

Maria took a deep breath. "I used to feel that way about this place too," she said hesitantly, "when I first came here. And it's easy to feel like an outsider even now. But it's not true." She took a step forward. "When I get to feeling sorry for myself, I think about my friends, my real friends who live here in Sweet Valley, kids who aren't jerks and losers at all. Kids like Elizabeth and Sophia." Folding her arms, she continued. "Friends can make the difference, Marshall. And I'd like to be your friend. If you give me another

Elizabeth Wakefield and Sophia Rizzo please come up to the stage?"

"That's us!" Sophia gave Elizabeth a shove.

Us? Elizabeth licked her lips nervously as she walked onto the stage, where she stood looking at Byron—but mostly looking at Todd.

Byron grinned at Elizabeth. "Elizabeth, meet Todd. Todd, meet Elizabeth. You've learned an important lesson today, kids. Now lead us in a dance." He turned to Sophia. "And the same goes for you, young lady. Always remember: There's no faking chemistry."

"Todd." Elizabeth fumbled for words. She looked into his clear eyes. "I'm—I'm sorry, Todd."

With trembling hands, Elizabeth pulled the teddy bear out from behind her back and handed it to Todd, together with the photo of them from the game room. "Remember these?" she asked. "From the one time all day when you thought you knew me."

Todd began to smile. "I sure do," he said. "Oh, Elizabeth, I'm glad you're back."

The band struck up a new, romantic song. Byron gave them a push. "Dance, guys," he whispered in their ears.

Elizabeth felt herself being led to the dance floor. All around her she could see other couples pairing off and joining them: Sophia and Patrick, Amy and Aaron, Byron and Jessica. Even Donald and Janet.

But she only had eyes for Todd.

No doubt about it—this was the best Valentine's Day ever.

chance, I'll help make you feel welcome."

"Great," Marshall muttered, but Maria thought he seemed more sad than angry now. "With friends like Sophia and you, who just say nasty things—"

"That was then," Maria said. "Things are different now."

"Sure, that's easy to say." Marshall tossed the book aside. "What makes things so *different* now?"

Maria took another deep breath. "I guess I'll have to tell you the truth," she said reluctantly. "Um . . . you see . . . we thought you were—" She broke off, wondering how to put it.

"Thought I was what?" Marshall demanded.

"A spy," Maria said softly. "We thought you were a spy, trying to prove that Patrick and Sophia cheated on the show. So that's why we were mean to you. But we just found out that you aren't a spy after all, so—"

"A *spy*?" Marshall interrupted. He sat up straight. "You thought I was a *spy*?"

"Well . . . yeah," Maria said heavily. Though now that she thought about it, she couldn't figure out how she could ever have believed Sophia. Marshall clearly wasn't the spy type. "I—I'm really sorry, Marshall. I should never have—"

"Cool!" Marshall's face burst into a big grin. "Me, a spy! That is so neat!" He bounced up out of the seat. "I've always wanted to be, you know, mysterious and cloak-and-daggery, but no one ever takes me seriously. They just say, 'Oh, Marshall, quit being weird.' But *you* guys thought I was a *spy!*" He extended his hand to Maria. "Thanks a lot!"

"Quiet down back there," Ms. Sylvester observed pointedly. "*Some* of us are trying to get our beauty sleep."

"Um, you're welcome," Maria told him. She was completely surprised by Marshall's response. Here she'd thought he'd hate her for sure, and instead he was flattered. "Glad we could . . ." *Be of help*, she finished in her mind, but decided not to say it out loud.

"You know what this reminds me of?" Marshall asked, grabbing her hand. "Did you ever see . . . well, you probably didn't." He thought about it for a minute. "Well, maybe you did, since you were in Hollywood and everything. Did you ever see that great film with Luke Maddock, the one where everybody thinks he's a spy, only he isn't?"

Maria opened her eyes wide. "You mean *Code Name: Anonymous*?" she asked with excitement.

"Yeah!" Marshall broke into the biggest grin Maria had ever seen. "You've seen it!"

"Like, five or six times!" Maria leaned forward, her hand still in Marshall's grasp. Her heart was beating double time. "Listen, Mr. Spy. I just had an idea. Let's finish our conversation to music, OK? Let's go on over to the dance. I promise no one will bite you."

Marshall grinned his lopsided grin. "I guess I'll take you up on that," he said shyly.

So it all worked out, Jessica thought dreamily, dancing in Byron's arms later that evening. The gym was beautifully decorated, the band was terrific, and when you came right down to it, she'd had a wonderful day.

The best Valentine's Day ever.

Todd and Elizabeth had gotten back together. So had Sophia and Patrick. Even Maria was looking cheerful now, dancing with Marshall (who kept stepping on her feet) and chattering about old movies that no one but them had ever heard of. And as for Donald and Janet . . .

"T minus ten seconds and counting," Byron hissed in her ear.

Jessica smiled. "Are you quoting Ms. Sylvester or something?"

Byron laid a finger to his lips. "The special-effects staff prepared a treat for you guys today, that's all. Five seconds. Watch."

The band played three final chords. Kids drifted apart, applauding.

"Now," Byron said.

There was a faint pop. Jessica looked up. Above her head, high on the ceiling of the gym, a fan began to whir, and clouds of pink fog puffed down toward the dancers below.

"It's beautiful!" she murmured.

Byron patted her shoulder. "And that's not all," he told her. "Keep watching!"

Jessica stared. Through the fog she saw little flashes of color. Long white streamers, pink balloons, and red paper hearts whirled down onto the floor and the stage. It was like a snowstorm, only a Valentine snowstorm instead of a real one.

"That's the other thing about love," Byron said, smiling. "We always want that happy ending. And here it is!"

A happy ending for everyone. Jessica smiled and lifted her face up to the ceiling. Little bits of red and pink floated down around her. She breathed deeply, enjoying the moment.

No Valentine's Day could possibly have been any better.

"Good morning, everyone!" Jessica chirped as she bounced into the kitchen the following Monday morning.

"What are you so happy about?" her brother Steven asked suspiciously. "I thought you hated Monday mornings."

"Not this Monday," Jessica said with a smile. "Isn't it a beautiful day?"

Elizabeth looked outside as a bolt of lightning flashed overhead. The sky was practically pitch black with freezing rain. She waited for the thunder to finish rumbling before saying dryly, "Gorgeous."

Steven's spoonful of oatmeal stopped halfway to his lips. "Who are you and what have you done with my sister?" he demanded.

Jessica flipped her hair and sat down. "Don't be silly, Steven. I'm just in a good mood, that's all. I happen to be excited about today's Unicorn meeting."

"Why?" Steven asked, a teasing note in his voice. "Do you have some hot new makeup tips to share?"

"I'll bet Jessica can't wait to talk about the fantastic Valentine's Day dance and how she got to dance with Byron Miller," Elizabeth guessed.

"Well, yes, I do want to talk about that," Jessica admitted. She took a sip of orange juice and continued. "But I also can't wait to point out to Lila that she's not the only one who's been to Dizzy Planet anymore. So she can stop bragging about having been there." Jessica thought for a moment. "Of course, being Lila, she'll probably have something else to brag about," she added. "It's a lucky thing we're friends, or else she'd really drive me crazy."

"It's too late for that," Steven joked.

"You can't bother me on such a wonderful day, Steven," Jessica said with a smile, and dug into her oatmeal. *Now that Lila can't brag anymore,* she thought, *it really will be wonderful!*

Elizabeth is determined to teach Jessica a lesson about lying. But when Elizabeth starts telling nothing but the truth, Jessica's life gets turned upside down! Can Jessica stop Elizabeth's pathological honesty before it drives everyone in Sweet Valley crazy? Find out in Sweet Valley Twins Super #11, **Jessica's No Angel.**

Lila Fowler is the girl who has everything—or is she? Find out what Lila's been missing in Sweet Valley Twins #115, **Happy Mother's Day, Lila.**

Bantam Books in the SWEET VALLEY TWINS series.
Ask your bookseller for the books you have missed.

3/88   7879

SIGN UP FOR THE SWEET VALLEY HIGH® FAN CLUB!

Hey, girls! Get all the gossip on Sweet Valley High's® most popular teenagers when you join our fantastic Fan Club! As a member, you'll get all of this really cool stuff:

- Membership Card with your own personal Fan Club ID number
- A Sweet Valley High® Secret Treasure Box
- Sweet Valley High® Stationery
- Official Fan Club Pencil (for secret note writing!)
- Three Bookmarks
- A "Members Only" Door Hanger
- Two Skeins of J. & P. Coats® Embroidery Floss with flower barrette instruction leaflet
- Two editions of *The Oracle* newsletter
- Plus exclusive Sweet Valley High® product offers, special savings, contests, and much more!

Be the first to find out what Jessica & Elizabeth Wakefield are up to by joining the Sweet Valley High® Fan Club for the one-year membership fee of only $6.25 each for U.S. residents, $8.25 for Canadian residents (U.S. currency). Includes shipping & handling.

Send a check or money order (do not send cash) made payable to "Sweet Valley High® Fan Club" along with this form to:

SWEET VALLEY HIGH® FAN CLUB, BOX 3919-B, SCHAUMBURG, IL 60168-3919

NAME_____
(Please print clearly)

ADDRESS_____

CITY_____ STATE _____ ZIP_____
(Required)

AGE _____ BIRTHDAY_____ /_____ /_____